OTHER WORKS BY A.M. RYCROFT

THE CATHELL SERIES

The Fall of Tynan Selvantyr
Into the Darkness
The Taming
The Joy Thief
Shadowboxer (The Gathering Dark, Pt. 1)

THE FALL OF KINGDOMS

Corruption of Honor
Pt. I: The Burning of Riverend
Pt. II: The Crow and The Butterfly
Pt. III: The Divide

Corruption of Honor

Pt. I

The Burning of Riverend

Corruption of Honor

Pt. I

The Burning of Riverend

A.M. RYCROFT

PITTSBURGH

Corruption of Honor et. al. © 2014-2017 A.M. Rycroft
Cover art and map © 2017, 2018 A.M. Rycroft
Edited by Juliet Bresler (Casa Cielo Editing), Eric Keizer

The "M" and quill design is a trademark of Mighty Quill Books, a subsidiary of Mighty, LLC.

First Printing: 2018

ISBN 978-1-7320013-2-9

Mighty Quill Books
www.mightyquillbooks.com

Special discounts are available on quantity purchases. For details, contact the publisher by email at info@mightyquillbooks.com or at the following address:

Mighty Quill Books
c/o Mighty, LLC.
370 Castle Shannon Blvd., 10366
Pittsburgh, PA 15234

To Erin —
My thanks for putting up with me, and Shaun, through the writing of this novel. You kept me as sane as I could be.

AUTHOR'S NOTE

The events in this book take place decades after the civil war known as the Nine Years War brought down old Empire and the Ten Kingdoms was formed from the ashes.

For a short history of the war and the realm, see the notes at the back of this book.

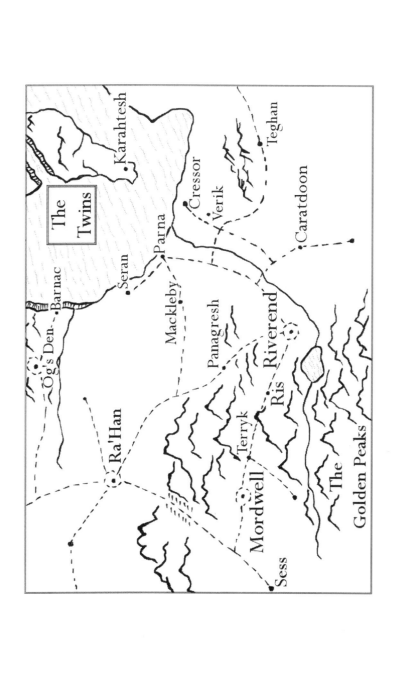

Watchers are expected to give their lives for the life of their Ward, without question.

Anything less is treason.

I

THE LAND held its breath, waiting. Bitter blackness, deeper than the night, crept in from the fields beyond the high gates of Riverend. It drowned the light from the stars and the full moon.

Soldiers on the western wall shuddered with the sudden drop in temperature, uncharacteristic even for the late summer. Then the torches around them began to die, one by one.

2

SHAUN resisted the urge to pace. Too many eyes watched her, all of them searching for signs of her guilt. Even the vaulted ceilings above seemed to press down on her in silent judgment.

She refused to give them what they wanted. She stood straight, her back pressed against the cool stone wall. Her hands rested lightly on the clasp of the sword belt at her waist.

Her dark eyes stared down the lantern-lit academy corridor, past those watching her—most of them students, a few of them court goers. She tried to focus her mind on looking for Sara. But though she could ignore their stares, she could not block out their whispering.

Betrayal. Shaun's insides twisted tighter each time it was repeated.

What happened was not her fault. She went where her training officer told her to go. It was *Sara* who asked that Shaun be removed as her Watcher—all over a stupid fight—as was Sara's right as the king's youngest daughter. But she could not then be angry at Shaun for who she was reassigned to. Not even when it was Darcy Krieger, Sara's greatest rival.

The gods must have had a good laugh over that.

Being tossed aside by her best friend must not have been humiliation enough.

Anger mixed with the sickness inside. Shaun let her head hang, trying to silence the sound of Darcy's laughter in her head.

Given the heated—and rather public—argument she had with Sara, followed by Darcy's display just a day later, Shaun could not really blame anyone for thinking she had switched her loyalties out of anger. Now thanks to Darcy's little prank, her position as a Watcher was in as much danger as her friendship with Sara. It did not matter that Shaun was at the top of her class of apprentice knights. Darcy had made the politics of the situation too toxic for anyone to leave it alone.

Shaun combed her calloused fingertips through the light brown hair that fell to the top of the collar of her pale tunic. Riverend's green and gray standard stood on one side of the low collar and the crest of the Knights Service on the other. Unconsciously, she tugged the collar straight and took in a steadying breath, drawing in the musty smell of the academy.

Sara could help her. She just needed to assure Sara that none of the rumors were true. If Sara showed up . . .

The evening's reading by some traveling poet was the kind of thing Shaun hated, but Sara loved. And yet, Sara was nowhere to be found, inside or outside the lecture hall. Shaun wondered if Sara had decided to skip the reading to avoid her. Sara had been acting so strange toward her of late.

Then Shaun spotted Sara turning the corner into the main corridor. She walked ahead of a group of friends, head down. The lantern light danced off the bejeweled clips in her blond hair. She walked with one of her favorite journals pressed to the front of her green silk dress like a shield.

Guilt suddenly overwhelmed Shaun. Perhaps what happened with Darcy was not her fault, but she should have anticipated a trick from the outset. She had been so blinded by her own hurt and humiliation, she never saw it coming.

For an instant, she considered turning the other way and leaving the academy before Sara saw her. Then her eyes lighted on the person walking next to Sara.

Jak.

His nose still hooked to the right where she broke it during the Trials. Above his trim ginger moustache and beard, it made his face look vaguely misaligned. Their rivalry was as well known as Darcy's with Sara.

Why was he with her? The answer came to her as soon as she asked herself the question: he was Shaun's replacement. The realization stung as sharply as if she had been slapped.

Before Shaun could stop herself, she moved to intercept them, speaking quickly. "Sara, I need to—"

Sara stopped. "No. Not a word, Shaun."

They were only a few months apart in age, but Shaun stood half a head taller. The anger and hurt in Sara's eyes, however, stopped her dead. Shaun forgot everything she wanted to say. Everything she had rehearsed over and over in her head just disappeared.

Silence hung heavy in the air between them.

Jak spoke first. "Princess, you do not want to miss the start of the reading." A smug smile stretched across his face. His eyes locked with Shaun's. One hand rested on the pommel of his sword, as if he expected her to challenge him in the middle of the corridor.

Before Shaun could respond, Sara nodded and stepped around her, heading into the lecture hall with Jak. A hand touched Shaun's shoulder. She spun around to see another of Sara's friends, Myra, standing behind her.

She smiled at Shaun. "Just give her some time."

Shaun sighed. "It didn't happen the way everyone— the way Darcy—is saying it did. I need her to know that."

The rest of Sara's friends exchanged skeptical looks.

Backbiting gossips. At nineteen summers now, about to enter her fifth year as an apprentice knight, their incessant desire for court gossip and rumors felt childish.

Myra nodded in sympathy, but said, "Just give her a day or two. She'll come around, and you can explain then."

"That is too long. Perhaps you could—"

Myra started shaking her head. "I don't think that is wise."

As usual, Myra would not take sides. She took her cues on how to navigate Sara and Shaun's arguments from her father, Riverend's highest diplomat. Though the arguments between Shaun and Sara had grown more frequent of late, Myra never gave up her neutral ground.

Another young woman leaned toward Myra and said quietly, "We should go inside and find seats."

Myra nodded. She told Shaun, "It will all work out. As it always does." She gave Shaun's arm a gentle squeeze, then turned away to enter the lecture hall.

All but Myra's Watcher, Thomas, went in with her. He turned an inquisitive look on Shaun. Thomas was her closest friend in the Knights Service.

She bit her lip. "What do I do?"

"Your choices are pretty clear: let it go or try to fix it now." He passed a hand over his close-cropped dark hair, then shrugged his broad shoulders. "Either carries risk. I cannot decide for you. You must do that."

He cocked his head and raised an eyebrow. "So decide which is more important. Outside or in?" Before she could answer, Thomas left her, too, going into the lecture hall after Myra.

Shaun stared at the open doorway. Myra was probably right, but giving Sara a few days to calm down required a kind of patience Shaun did not possess.

A rumble of thunder reached her from outside the academy hall, and suddenly, a sharp sense of foreboding passed over her. She ignored it, however, and walked toward the lecture hall doors.

3

SOLDIERS huddled in tight groups on the western wall, staring out into the still darkness around them. Their grips tightened on their swords and pole arms. None dared speak higher than a whisper.

A deep rumble of thunder caused a lamb somewhere in the pasture beyond the capital's gates to let out a fearful bleat. A few soldiers jumped at the sound. The others let out nervous chuckles at their jumpiness.

Then a deafening buzz, like the approach of a thousand locusts, filled the air. The men and women on the wall cried out and clapped hands over their ears.

Angry forks of red lightning cut across the sky over the main road that wove through the pastureland beyond the western gate. A sharp thunderclap followed, melding with the buzzing sound for a moment. The wall shuddered under the soldiers' feet with the force of the boom. Soldiers shouted and grabbed hold of the battlements to keep from pitching over.

A second blast of lightning shot from the sky, arcing down toward the road. Its brightness momentarily blinded the onlookers. Just as the afterimage faded, an army of no less than five hundred men materialized on the road where the lighting had struck, only a hundred paces from the city gates.

The wall guard stared down at the army, wondering if they were nothing more than an illusion. Then archers stepped to the front of the army's ranks and launched a swift volley of arrows up at those staring dumbly atop the wall.

Riverend soldiers scattered as the arrows flew. Those not fast enough to take cover behind the battlements' merlons fell as the arrows hit their marks. The rest of the ranks below let loose a bloodthirsty howl and charged the gates.

4

SHAUN stopped short of the lecture hall entrance. Two of the king's guard just stood inside, to the left and right of the doors, reminding her that King Jaris himself was inside. She could not just charge in without drawing his attention, the last thing she wanted. The foreboding inside her doubled.

As the only child of Jaris's guard master, he had treated Shaun like a member of his own family from the time she was born. But Jaris Hahlerand had no patience for being pulled into arguments between her and Sara. She would need to keep from drawing his attention. She could not give anyone yet another reason to cut her from the Knights Service.

The king stood at the front of the hall, near the lectern at its center. His tall, broad frame and thick beard had always made him seem to her like he was kith and kin to a great bear. The gray that had overtaken his hair in recent years had not lessened this image for her.

An elderly man—the poet, Shaun assumed— stood with the king, conversing quietly. The older man appeared hunchbacked, bent forward at a severe angle. Even if he was to stand straight, she doubted he would stand any taller than the king's shoulder and yet his dark robes pooled around his feet.

Shaun shifted to look up the rows of carved wooden benches rising up to the back of the lecture hall. People passing through the entrance ahead of her kept blocking her view, making it impossible for her to find Sara from where she stood. She ducked inside and headed for the steps on the outside of the rows.

King Jaris suddenly barked out a deep laugh. Shaun jumped and looked over her shoulder, then breathed a sigh of relief. The king's attention remained focused on the old man.

She continued up to the topmost row. Sara was easier for her to pick out from there. She sat just a few rows up from the front of the hall, too close to the king for Shaun's comfort.

Jak crouched next to Sara. He said something to her and twisted his face into a goofy grin. To Shaun's horror, Sara smiled back. *Worse*, she looked interested in what he was saying.

Shaun resisted the urge to charge down the rows and shove him down the steps. Instead she crouched behind the row of people in front of her. She chewed at her thumbnail and considered her next move.

Her mother's voice in her head needled at her. It told her that if she kept chewing on her nails, she was apt to get an ingrown nail. Then how would she hold her sword?

Shaun sighed and let her hand drop. But she was no archer like her mother, who kept her nails neat and trim. The wall was not where she belonged, like it was for her mother and father. Her place was at Sara's side.

The place Jak occupied now.

She straightened the collar on her cream-colored

tunic. The difference in color from the dark gray worn by other apprentice knights marked her as a Watcher. Sara's Watcher. That was who she was.

Standing again, Shaun readjusted her sword belt. She took the stairs two at a time until she stood behind Jak. She glanced at Sara, but when Sara looked up at her, her smile faded into a frown.

Not good.

Jak turned to look at Shaun as well. "Do you need something?"

"I need you to find somewhere else to be."

"I am assigned to Sara today. I'm not going anywhere."

Shaun's jaw tightened. She crouched down to his level and kept her voice low. "And what a fantastic job you're doing, too, sitting here cracking jokes with her." His mouth fell open to protest, but she cut him off. "Be on your way, before I call the king over and tell him what a great job you're doing flirting with his daughter."

Jak's jaw snapped shut. He scowled at her, nostrils flaring. "I will go, but my training officer will hear about this." He got up and stalked off.

Shaun watched him leave. She did not doubt his conviction but decided she would worry about him later. She sat in the empty space next to Sara on the carved wooden bench.

Sara avoided her eye, instead staring down at the journal in her lap. Her dark blond hair cascaded in gentle waves over the shoulders of her dress, the locks tamed only by matching green ribbons and hair clips shaped like butterflies.

The angry furrow in Sara's brow stood in direct conflict to the butterflies' cheerfulness. "That was rude,

Shaun." Her fingers crimped the journal's corners. "You should not have come tonight."

"I needed to talk to you." Shaun quickly smoothed back the strands of hair trying to fall in her eyes.

"I thought—" Sara paused, but then she seemed to think better of what she was about to say.

Had Sara been about to say she expected Shaun to be at Darcy's side instead? Could Sara believe that of her, after all their years of friendship?

Sara crossed her arms. "I made it plain last night that I did not want to see you today. I had hoped you would respect that request. Nothing has changed. If anything, I want to see you even less now."

"Whatever they're saying about what happened this afternoon is not true. It's just gossip. Lies."

Sara flicked her eyes in Shaun's direction. She could not read what was in them. "Are you denying that Darcy had her arm in yours? And that you were laughing with her as though you've been friends forever. Those things are not true?"

A frown crept on to Shaun's face. She spoke carefully. "Yes, Darcy insisted on putting her arm in mine while we walked in the park—"

"Our favorite part of that park."

"—and she tripped in the grass. I may have laughed when I caught her." Shaun paused. "I don't remember now." The little white lie slipped out before she could stop it.

Darcy had "tripped" right when they were passing a group of Sara's cousins and their friends. Shaun laughed out of surprise when Darcy collided with her. She could not be sure the collision was purposeful, but she almost ended up in the grass with Darcy.

She just barely kept her feet and then Darcy started laughing, too. Much louder than the situation warranted. She saw Darcy glance at Sara's cousins to make sure they were watching, then put her hand on Shaun's shoulder. Just that small gesture of familiarity had no doubt sealed Shaun's guilt in the minds of those watching.

"It was all a farce made up by Darcy to drive a wedge between you and me," Shaun insisted. "We weren't telling each other jokes as we walked, no matter what Darcy or your cousins may say."

But the angry furrow in Sara's brow persisted. "Why were you walking in that part of the park?"

A lesser minister's son sitting in front of them turned to Shaun and interrupted before she could answer. "Excuse me. Might I ask you to kindly hold this argument until after the reading is over? When you're somewhere the rest of us cannot hear you?"

Shaun felt a snide comment trying to fight its way out but contained it. She nodded at the young man. He was probably right. She could feel herself headed down the same path with Sara as the night before. Better to stop now before she got herself in more trouble. Maybe Sara would listen to reason later.

The young man gave her a tight smile and faced forward again. When Shaun turned to look at Sara, however, Sara turned her face away, ignoring her. Myra's voice echoed through Shaun's head, telling her again to just let Sara have time.

Shaun sighed and looked down toward the lectern. The poet was shuffling some scrolls. The king gestured for the guards by the doors to shut them and made his way toward an empty place in the second row.

She glanced at Sara again, who was still ignoring her. Perhaps Sara wished Jak was next to her instead, making his stupid little jokes. Indignation burned its way back to the surface. She pressed her lips into a thin line and leaned toward Sara.

"I go where I am ordered to go. Darcy chose the spot for us to walk, not I. You and she can order your Watchers to go where you like, and we must comply. And you and she can request whoever you want as your Watchers. So I'll ask, did you purposely request Jak as Darcy requested me?"

Sara said nothing, but Shaun caught Sara's subtle flinch when she asked the question. Even though she knew the answer before she asked, all the air rushed out of her at once. A sharp pain stabbed her in the gut as though she had been punched.

Her mouth felt numb as she said, "I cannot believe you would do that. Knowing how I feel about him."

The young man in front of Shaun coughed lightly and glanced back again.

Sara leaned forward and gave him the same tight-lipped smile he had given Shaun. "My apologies, Joffrey, but perhaps you could keep your eyes pointed ahead and mind your own affairs."

Joffrey frowned but turned to face forward again.

Sara glared at Shaun. "Do not try to make this about what I did. You do not see me, Shaun. But Jak does. He does not tell me I am foolish for worrying about my studies or tell me I spend too much time fussing with my hair, like you do. And he does not act friendly towards someone who has always hated me—for gods-only-know-what reason."

"Act friendly—with *Darcy*? Are you serious?" Shaun glared back. Angry words came pouring out. "You think that Jak is your friend? He's nice to you because you are the king's daughter. It is his job to be kind to you and take care of you."

Sara's lips parted in shock.

"And the fact that you are a beautiful young woman only gives him another reason to seek your favor."

The moment the words left her mouth, Shaun regretted them. Tears stood out in Sara's eyes and her lip quivered for just a moment. In that moment, Shaun's anger dissipated and she felt shame.

Why did this keep happening between them? When had they become so antagonistic to each other?

Sara whispered, "How dare you." She wiped away her tears and stood up. She repeated the words, more loudly. "How dare you, Shaun. Stay here if you like. I will leave instead." She turned away.

Without thinking, Shaun grabbed Sara's wrist. *"Wait—"*

Sara spun back and yanked free of Shaun's grip, nearly shouting, *"You are out of bounds, knight."*

The look on Sara's face bordered on hatred. Startled, Shaun pulled her hand back. Then she noticed that the entire hall had fallen silent. From the front of the room, the king cleared his throat.

5

THE HOWLING outside the wall and the boom of the portcullis falling over the heavy inner gates shook Tor Greyson awake from where he had dozed off at his desk in the western guard tower. The guards master snapped up his sword belt and sprinted down the steps, holding to the rough stone walls as he descended. Just as he ran out of the tower, arrows streaked through the air, raining down around him. He dove behind a high merlon for cover.

Others around him were not so lucky. The arrows struck their marks with impossible accuracy. The wounded and dying toppled around him. Some called his name, but he dared not move, even to pull whomever he could to safety.

He could smell the stink of dark magiks in the air. *Mordwell.*

A green flash appeared from below, where the wood and iron portcullis stood. Something crashed into it. Smoke billowed up and over the sides of the battlements. Panic rose in him. They were going to get through.

Tor shouted over the cries around him. "Get to the holes!"

Archers scrambled for the murder holes in the parapet and the walkway, firing down at the invaders. He did not know how many Mordwellians were out there, but they were not going to get to the inner gate without challenge.

As soon as the Mordwellian arrows stopped flying, Tor shot forward and pulled a wounded man back toward the cover of the parapet. "What happened?"

The man coughed up blood and shook his head. "I don't know, sir. There was this flash of lightning and then scores of soldiers in black armor appeared outside the gates."

"How many—"

A series of pops and shrieks from the direction of the holes cut him off. Archers fell to the stone walkway, clawing at their burned faces. The rest fell back in horror.

Tor stared at them, his mind going back to a time when he saw the very same thing, when his father was Guards Master as he was now. It was happening again.

Something heavier than the magik blast slammed into the iron-banded inner doors, shaking the wall again. *Battering ram.*

He pulled himself from his memories. "Sound the—"

A second collision drowned out his orders. Crackling wood accompanied the second boom, but the doors held. It would not be long before they gave way. The Mordwellians could not burn through the inner door, so they would batter their way through instead.

"Blast them all." He shouted again, "Sound the alarms! Turn out everyone we have! Archers to the inner parapet. They're comin' through."

Soldiers at arms scrambled to pull the wounded men and women out of the way of the archers taking position along the inside edge of the wall. Others descended to the ground level to turn out the rest of the guard. He grabbed one of the soldiers running past.

"Find my wife on the north wall. Tell her 'The Burning is happening again.'"

She looked confused. "The *what*, sir?"

He shook his head. "Just tell her what I said. And make sure someone finds the king. We're under siege by Mordwell."

Her mouth fell open, but she asked him no more questions before she ran for the ladders. The great bells atop the guard towers started clanging to alert the city and the villages beyond the wall. The warning was too late though.

Tor pressed his fingers to his ears to block out the deafening peal of the bells and thought of his daughter. He was old enough to remember the Nine Years War. He knew what was to come.

He regretted that he and his wife had kept the stories about the war from Shaun, the ones the academy did not tell the students. They always thought there was time for that later, if even it was to come again. Without any idea of where in the city Shaun might be, he had no way to warn her.

Another boom sounded from below, followed by cracking wood and squealing metal as the doors gave up against the battering ram. Tor drew in a steadying breath and unsheathed his sword.

Shaun was not ready for what was about to happen. He prayed the gods would have mercy on her.

6

SARA'S face paled at the same time as fear tightened in Shaun's chest. The king stared up at them from where he stood, just two rows down, his arms crossed over his broad chest. Shaun suddenly wished the floor would open up and swallow her, or that the gods would finally take pity and smite her where she sat.

Jaris's voice boomed across the silent hall. "Sara Hahlerand and Shaundra Greyson! Are we intruding on your argument?"

Sara dropped her gaze. Shaun bowed her head in deference and to hide her burning cheeks before she fell awkwardly to one knee on the steps.

"Your Majesty, my sincerest apologies for the disruption. I take full responsibility."

The king said nothing at first, and his disapproval hung heavy in the air. Pinpricks of sweat stood out on her forehead as she waited for him to order her out of the lecture hall.

The king finally commanded her, "Stand up, Shaun."

She got to her feet and stood at attention.

"Our honored guest has traveled to our fair capital from well afar. I think we owe him the courtesy of *quiet* while he reads for us. Agreed?"

The king arched an eyebrow at her, but she caught the hint of a smile curling a corner of his lips. Was it her nervousness that amused him or something else?

"Yes, Sire."

"Good. Then let us take our seats, so we may stop wasting the good man's time." His eyes went to his daughter. "*All* of us."

Sara must have given him an earful regarding the rumors about her and Darcy, and he was done with it. He turned his back on them and sat down. Sara and Shaun did the same. The poet, however, never got the chance to read after all.

An immense *boom* shook the academy building. Several people cried out in surprise. Pealing bells suddenly filled the air as a dozen alarms around the city all began ringing at once. Shaun froze. This was no drill. Something terrible had happened.

The doors to the lecture hall banged open and a blood-covered knight spilled through them. "Your Majesty! The gates have been breached. We are under siege by Mordwell!" She fell forward into the arms of the nearest of the king's guard.

The room erupted with many voices speaking all at once. Shaun, other apprentice knights, and the full knights in attendance jumped to their feet.

The king shouted, "*Silence*. Remain calm!"

The poet started giggling. "More than just the walls have been breached, King Jaris. How fortuitous that you could join us this evening."

All eyes turned to him. He suddenly shifted from an old man into a much taller, younger man. Wild zeal filled his eyes. He lifted his hands. Shaun's hand fell to her sword's hilt.

Before anyone could move to stop him, the man shouted a word Shaun did not understand. A white-hot fireball formed in his open hand. He hurled it in the king's direction. One of the knights nearest the king knocked him out of its path, sacrificing himself to the assassin's spell.

People in the rows in front of her screamed as the fireball's energies exploded outward on impact. Shaun dove at Sara, knocking her to the floor and covering her, just before the wave of heat and flames washed up the rows. She clenched her teeth as the heat singed her bare forearms and the back of her neck.

When the heat had dissipated, Shaun sat up to make sure Sara was alright and immediately gagged on the smells of burning wood and burnt flesh. Thick black smoke rose from where the fireball had landed. People screamed in pain. Knights and guardsmen shouted for the king.

From somewhere in the thick smoke, he answered, "I'm fine! Get that bastard before he does any more damage."

Shaun yanked her dagger free from where it was strapped to her boot and searched for the sorcerer's position through the smoke and debris floating in the air. She caught sight of him just as he raised his arm to throw another fireball.

She hurled her dagger at the sorcerer's throat. It lodged in his chest instead, landing with a dull thud and choking off his spell before he could finish. The nascent fireball exploded in his hand, sending out another wave of heat and light. Shaun shielded her eyes.

When she looked again, the sorcerer had fallen back against the wall. Much of his arm and the sleeves and chest of his robes were gone. Only charred flesh remained. Surprisingly, the sorcerer still moved, seemingly unaware of the extent of his injuries.

"Grab him," the king ordered.

The king's guard surrounded the dying sorcerer. Shaun followed behind the king.

The sorcerer's breath wheezed in and out through scarred lips wet with blood. He did not struggle against the guards who pulled him to his feet, but he forced a grin onto his burned face when the king came to stand in front of him.

"Did you like Mordwell's surprise?" He coughed and more blood bubbled out of his mouth.

The king growled, "*Treacherous bastards.* My father should have wiped the House of Mackritae off the face of Decathea twenty years ago when he had the chance."

The sorcerer laughed. "So like the House of Hahlerand to revise history in its favor. Your father was a *fool.* He could not best us. We have the upper hand now."

"After so long since signing the accord, why would the Mackritae launch another war now?"

"Because the Mackritae are gone," the sorcerer hissed. "They no longer hold us back."

Jaris bent closer to the sorcerer. "Whomever your masters are now, I will snuff them out."

He grabbed hold of Shaun's dagger and yanked it from the sorcerer's burned chest. Blood ran from the hole the dagger left behind. The sorcerer's eyes and mouth widened and then his eyes rolled back in his head.

Jaris handed the dagger back to Shaun. The hilt was still warm. She almost dropped it in surprise.

The king's guard let the sorcerer's body slump to the

floor. She stared at him a moment. She had never watched someone die. It was nothing so simple as what she had imagined.

Riverend foot soldiers and more knights poured into the lecture hall. Knights Master Farrash came in with them. One of the knights already in the lecture hall shouted for everyone to come to attention. Shaun forced herself to turn away from the dead man and snapped to attention with the other apprentice knights, hands at her sides. She tried to ignore the blood growing sticky on the dagger's hilt.

"At ease," Farrash ordered them.

She relaxed and wiped what blood she could get off her dagger blade against the shin of her leather leggings. Then she slipped it back into its scabbard.

Farrash addressed the king, "Your Majesty, we have reports that five hundred Mordwellians appeared from nowhere outside the western gate. They broke through with their dark magiks."

Father. Shaun prayed he was alright.

"They obliterated many of our defenses before we knew what was happening. The city may fall despite our best efforts. We must get you to safety."

King Jaris shook his head. "I will not let these villains chase me from my city just yet. The rest, though, must flee now."

The king pulled himself up to his full height and a calm settled over him that Shaun envied. Her thoughts raced as she tried to make sense of what was happening. How could they be at war with Mordwell after so long? What had the sorcerer meant about the Mackritaes being gone?

Jaris faced the room. "Everyone, gather around."

Thomas and Myra came to stand near her. Sara stood next to her father.

"You must flee for now, but know that we will never fully abandon our kingdom to these blackguards. Apprentice knights, get your Wards and as many of our people as you can out of the city. That is your duty, and I expect you to carry it out to the very best of your abilities.

"I know few of you possess battle experience. You may think what I'm asking of you is beyond your reach, but I am confident it is not. I have faith in your strength.

"My knights, guardsmen, and I will battle the enemy as long as we can to help you get free. Split up into small groups for stealth and retreat in the direction of Parna to the east. I shall gather our reserve forces from the surrounding towns and we can regroup in Parna in two days' time. When we are at our strongest again, we will return to our capital city to give the Mordwellians a thrashing worthy of any bard's song."

The king turned to Shaun and laid a hand on her shoulder. "Shaun, you must take Sara from here and keep her safe."

Sara cried out, "No, Father! Please don't send me away." Tears fell down her cheeks. He cut off her protests with a shake of his head.

"Shaun, my daughter is your lone responsibility now. Do you understand? I expect you to give your life for hers, if you must."

Everything felt like it was moving too quickly for her to keep up, but Shaun nodded. "Yes, Sire. I pledge to give my life for hers."

"Good."

The king embraced Sara. Her shoulders shook as she sobbed softly against her father's chest. He did not hold her for long, however.

When he gently pushed her away again, he told her, "Go with Shaun and the others now. I will see you in Parna."

Sara begged him again, "Please do not send me away. I can be of use to you."

The king smiled at his favorite daughter, but there was worry in his eyes. "Nay. You are no fighter, and I must be strong for my people now. Shaun will keep you safe until we meet again. I'm ordering you to go with her."

"What about Mother?"

The king looked to Farrash. "My wife?"

"I've been told her guards escorted her to the tunnels as soon as the alarm sounded. I have no doubt she got safely away."

King Jaris nodded. "Very good. Someone bring me a sword."

A guardsman handed him the sword from his own sheath. Jaris looked at the apprentice knights. "I expect to see you all in Parna. Go now. Shaun, take the lead."

Shaun took a steadying breath and nodded. "Yes, Sire."

She motioned to Thomas and jogged to the lecture hall's entrance with him. They took up opposite points on either side of the doorway. She drew her sword, as did Thomas.

He poked his head out and looked down one end of the corridor and then the other. He nodded. The corridor was clear. Shaun gripped her sword tightly and stepped out into the passage.

7

SHAUN relaxed her grip on her sword's hilt once she stood in the still, empty corridor. She motioned to Thomas to send people out. With everyone gathered in the corridor, Shaun divided them into four groups, appointing Jak and two other Watchers as leaders.

"Take separate ways out of the academy. Once you're out, split again into groups of no more than four each for mobility and stealth."

The other Watchers murmured their agreement and led their groups away. Jak started past her, but she caught his arm.

He shot her an angry look. "Unhand me."

She let go but told him, "Don't die." She would not give Sara yet another reason to hate her.

Jak jabbed a finger into his chest. "I should be going with Sara, too. *I* was assigned as her Watcher."

She sniped back, "Only for a day." Then she closed her eyes and took a deep breath. "Look, the king ordered me to watch over Sara. You are a capable fighter and the others need you to lead them now. I expect you keep yourself alive while you're at it."

He sighed but gave her a curt nod.

Shaun nodded back and turned to her own group.

Thomas asked, "Which route shall we take?"

"Past the library. There is a hidden storeroom there that my father told me of once. We can get armor and more weapons inside. You take the rear guard."

She walked to where Sara stood with Myra. "I want you with me at the front of the group, in case we encounter resistance."

Sara met her eyes. Anger still hardened them. "I will stay with Myra."

Shaun's jaw tightened. They had no time to argue. "Myra can come with you to the front of the group, but you will stay near me so that I can do my job as your Watcher."

She spun on her heel without waiting for a response, gesturing for the rest to follow her. Once Sara and Myra reached the front of the group, she headed off in the direction of the academy library, moving as quickly as she dared through the corridors, knowing they would not stay empty for long.

Angry shouts and breaking glass from outside grew louder as they got closer to the library at the front of the academy hall. The Mordwellians would no doubt look inside the buildings for people to capture or kill. They needed to get to the storeroom before enemy soldiers found them.

Shaun stopped outside the heavy wooden doors of the library. She cracked one open and peered inside the dimly lit room. The smell of must and aging parchment that permeated much of the academy was strongest there.

Only one lantern remained alight, left behind on one of the wide tables standing at the center of the cavernous room. Likely, whomever had been studying the books still scattered across the table had fled when the alarms bells rang out.

The group filed in, their footsteps made silent by thick rugs piled on top of each other over the stone floors. They passed enormous rows of bookshelves crammed from top to bottom with tomes and scrolls. Shaun avoided looking at them as she headed to the back of the library.

She tried not to think of all the times she walked between the rows, letting her fingers trail along the smooth, wooden shelves and cracked leather spines. Many times had she paused to thumb through histories of famous knights while Sara sat at one of the broad library tables, concentrating on the studies that Shaun too often ignored. But such thoughts now only reminded her that she may never get the chance to do such a thing again if the Mordwellians had their way.

She counted the bookcases against the back wall until she came to the seventh one from the center. There was a gap on either side of it. She felt along both sides and found a groove where she could grip the shelf's edge and pull it forward. When she tried, however, it barely moved, the hidden door stiff from disuse. She tightened her grip and pulled harder. The bookcase moved outward only a little before it squealed to a stop. Cursing, she tugged at the bookcase with both hands. The door still refused to open more.

A fellow Watcher, Brekt, hissed at her from the direction of the library doors, "I can hear boots down the corridor."

Shaun called to Thomas, "Help me."

Both of them grabbed the edge of the bookcase. On the count of three, they pulled as one. Whatever held the door back finally let go and allowed them to swing it open.

The room beyond was pitch black, but Shaun ushered everyone in. She grabbed the handle on the back side of the bookcase and tugged it back into place behind her, cringing at the noise the bookcase made.

Thomas lit the lightstone he always carried in the pouch on his belt. It illuminated the small room from end to end. The room barely fit all of them, and the temperature started to rise within moments. Shaun brushed away the sweat beading on her forehead.

She crossed to Thomas's side, where he stood in front of racks that lined one side of the room, heavy with armor and weapons. Everything bore a thin layer of dust and most of the bladed weapons did not look sharp enough to be useful. The armor, however, looked to still be in decent condition. Very little rust dotted the metal surfaces.

Thomas passed pieces of armor to the other apprentice knights. Shaun took the mail shirt handed to her, but waved off a shield, instead taking a pair of scuffed bracers. Even with the leather straps pulled tight, they did not quite fit her wiry forearms, but they would have to do. She searched for Sara in the group.

She was huddled with Myra. She did not meet Shaun's eyes, but Shaun could see the worry etched on her face. No doubt she wondered about her father and whether he would make it to safety.

Shaun turned away. The king was someone else's responsibility. Sara was hers. The best she could was what she had been told: get Sara safely out of the city.

A lump rose in her throat as she thought of having to leave the capital, the only home she had ever known.

Shaun swallowed hard around it and cleared her throat.

She whispered to Thomas, "There should be a way out on the other side." She went to the opposite end of the room and ran her hands down the wall.

Her fingers found a panel cut in the false wall, close to the floor and just wide enough for one person to crawl through once it was opened. Its size would make checking for enemy soldiers harder than she would have liked, but they could not go back the way they came. Not with Mordwellians closing in on the library.

She crouched by the panel to press her ear to it. No sounds came through. She prayed that meant the corridor beyond was empty.

She turned back to the others and whispered to the apprentice knights, "Once we leave here, we split into smaller groups. Thomas, I want you and Myra to come with Sara and me. Kera and Andrin, divide up the rest of the group between yourselves."

Kera and Andrin agreed.

"Shaun." Myra came to stand near her. "I am worried about my parents and my little brother. Can we look for them before we leave Riverend?"

She did not look well, her pallor and shaking hands visible to Shaun even in the dim light. Worried was an understatement. She was terrified.

Shaun looked at Thomas, but he only met her eyes and said nothing. She looked at Sara behind Myra. But Sara said nothing either. Shaun sighed and pressed her lips into a thin line.

She shook her head. "We can't. We must find a way out of the city as soon as possible, or we may find all escape routes cut off to us. I know not where we might search for them. If they are not out of the city already, I'm afraid that they may be dead or prisoners of the Mordwellians."

Sara hissed, *"Shaun."*

Myra squeezed Sara's hand. "No, I understand." A quavering tone of desperation filled her voice. "But they would have been in the southern tower of the castle, where my family's quarters are. Please. Can we not at least search there? I cannot just abandon them."

"Yes, we can look for them," Sara said. The look she gave Shaun made it clear she would not hear any argument.

Shaun looked again at Thomas. He gave her a small shrug, saying, "The castle is on the way."

"Fine. There's an escape tunnel entrance near there. We can try to get out of the city through the tunnel after we look for Myra's family." She looked at Myra. "But if we encounter too much resistance before we reach the castle, I cannot risk Sara's life to reach your family."

Myra nodded.

Shaun turned back to the panel. She slid it open only a few fingers wide. Seeing no one immediately in front of it, she slid it open the rest of the way.

Still nothing. She stuck her head and shoulders out.

Rough hands suddenly grabbed her. Shaun yelped and Sara shrieked her name behind her. Shaun tried to twist free, but her assailant yanked her through the opening, into the corridor.

8

SHAUN's body collided with the opposite wall. She fell to the floor, stunned. Through a haze of sparkling lights, she registered her attacker hauling her up again. She came face-to-face with a soldier in black leather armor.

His skin was dead pale, and his eyes possessed a vacant quality and a vague milky hue that made Shaun think of something dead. His breathing wheezed strangely in his throat. Then the Mordwellian's face broke into a sinister grin. He slammed his forehead into hers.

The impact sent pain all the way down to her teeth, and stars exploded in her vision again. The Mordwellian made a rasping, laughing sound and kept her from sliding to the floor. Something wet—*his tongue*—slid up the side of her face. She cried out in disgust and tried to squirm away, but he held her fast. He licked the blood pouring down her face from where he struck her.

A loud cracking suddenly filled the corridor. The wall separating the hidden room and the corridor exploded outward. Thomas and two other apprentice knights fell out in a spray of broken wood and plaster. The rest of the apprentice knights ran out through the new opening, weapons at the ready. The Mordwellian dropped her.

Thomas ran to her side. "Are you alright?"

Her head throbbed as she sat up, but she nodded. He helped her to feet while the others slew the Mordwellian.

Pounding boots echoed down the corridor as additional Mordwellians arrived. Thomas drew his sword. He told her, "Just collect yourself a moment."

Thomas and the other apprentice knights formed a protective circle around her and the others. Shaun gripped the wall, leaning against it as she tried to shake the rhythmic throbbing in her head.

Sara touched her arm. "Hold still. You're hurt." Concern crept into her tone.

Shaun slowly shook her head, but it only made the throbbing worse. She muttered, "I'm fine."

"You are not. You're bleeding."

Metal sang and clashed as the Mordwellians met swords with Thomas and the other apprentice knights. The sound nearly drowned Sara out.

Shaun tried to push past her. "I need to join the others."

Myra stopped her. She produced a handkerchief and ordered her, "Hold still." She pressed it to the blood that still ran down Shaun's face and dabbed it away from her eyes. Then she nodded. "Alright. Go now."

Shaun drew her sword and joined the fight at Thomas's side. Although the enemy soldiers were outnumbered, they fought with an uncanny strength and speed. All displayed the same pallor as the one who attacked her. None of them spoke or made any sound other than the quiet wheezing.

The eerie sound and their pale skin reminded Shaun of the stories Riverend children told each other about Mordwell's walking dead. Her mother claimed it was nothing more than childish nonsense when she had asked.

But Shaun began to wonder if the stories were true after all. The Mordwellians did not succumb to blows that would incapacitate a human. Only running them through the chest or throat seemed to stop them.

When all five Mordwellians were finally dead, the apprentice knights regrouped and treated the injuries they had all sustained. Kera had received the worst of them, a deep gash across one of her thighs. Thomas and Shaun helped bind it for her, but she needed to lean on the others to walk.

Shaun frowned. Kera's injuries would slow her group down and make it easier for them to be captured. But they would have to make do. The group had to split up again.

As soon as everyone was bandaged and able to move on, the groups split off and went their separate ways. She led Thomas, Sara, and Myra in the direction of the main entrance. They met two more enemy soldiers along the way, but knowing how to kill them now, Shaun and Thomas dispatched them more quickly than the others. But any relief she felt ended when they exited the academy building.

The lampposts and torches that normally lit the city streets were all dark, but fires bathed the city in orange light. Everywhere she looked, she saw fighting. Even groups of civilians battled Mordwellians in the streets. Those not able to fight were dragged away screaming by enemy soldiers.

Shaun stared open-mouthed at the scene. Sara or Myra gasped behind her. She shook herself and murmured numbly that they had to keep moving.

Thomas suggested they take the alleys to reach the castle rather than the streets. He took the lead and guided them down a series of dark passages. They managed to skirt around much of the fighting. When they got within sight of the castle, however, it became obvious their detour had been as useless as Shaun had feared.

Flames licked out from multiple breaches in the western and southern walls of the castle. The top half of the western tower was gone, obliterated by some force. If Myra's family was inside when the tower was struck, they would have died in the blast.

"No!" Myra rushed past her, out of the alley.

Shaun and Thomas cursed in unison.

Myra ran toward the castle's curtain wall, shouting, *"Mother. Father. Jenik!"*

Sara started forward, but Shaun caught her arm. "No. Stay back here."

Thomas ran after Myra and grabbed her before she attracted the attention of any Mordwellian soldiers. She struggled against him, still screaming her brother's name. He shushed her and lifted her up in his strong arms.

When they reached the alley again, Myra had stopped screaming. She wept against Thomas's chest.

Sara stroked Myra's hair, trying to soothe her. "They may have gotten out. They may have."

Myra nodded, but said nothing.

Thick smoke swirled around the castle and blew back toward the alley, stinging Shaun's eyes. She coughed and said, "We have to find another way out. With the fires, we cannot safely reach the tunnels under the castle."

Thomas nodded. "Maybe there is a breach somewhere in the city wall."

She asked him quietly, "Can she walk?"

Myra murmured, "I'll be fine." She wiped her eyes,

now red with grief, and eased away from Thomas.

Shaun nodded and turned back the way they had come. At the nearest junction in the alleyway, she turned toward the eastern city wall. When they reached it, Shaun looked up, hoping to see her mother or father, but smoke from the fires obscured her view. She and the others followed the thick city wall, looking for a break. Wide cracks and burns marred areas of the wall, high and low. Whatever had destroyed part of the castle appeared to have struck the wall, too.

Several paces down, they found a long fissure and a gap where the stone blocks had cracked and crumbled away at the bottom. It was just wide enough for them to crawl through one at a time.

She frowned at the breach. The last time she squeezed through a hole in a wall had not gone so well. Her head still ached from the encounter.

Thomas looked at her, hands on his hips. His frown echoed hers. "I don't like tight spaces . . . But I'll go through first this time."

He handed his sword belt to her, muttering, "I don't want to get stuck."

"Be careful," Sara said, her arms wrapped around Myra. She shivered as a chill wind blew past the wall.

Thomas wormed his way into the long hole until his boots disappeared. Shaun looked around, making sure no one was watching. Thomas called out to her. She crouched down to look through.

"All clear."

She passed his sword to him and then helped Myra and Sara through the breach in the wall. Once they were safely through, Shaun tossed her sword to Thomas on the other side.

A voice boomed at her from behind, making her stop and turn. Her mouth fell open when she saw what at first appeared to be a hairy mountain running in her direction.

The giant closed the distance faster than she thought possible, given his bulk. His woolly beard flapped around his thick neck. Unlike the Mordwellians she fought in the academy corridors, he did not look half-dead. Wild zeal filled his eyes, just like the assassin in the lecture hall. He raised a massive double-bladed ax over his head as he ran.

If she tried to get into the hole now, she would lose both legs for sure. She waited until he got within striking range and dove to the side as the ax dropped. It whistled through empty air.

The Mordwellian growled and spun with the ax's momentum, trying to catch her as she got up. She cursed and pitched herself into a roll, just out of the ax's path.

Movement by the hole caught her attention. Thomas poked his head through and looked around for her. The giant saw him at the same time as she did. He laughed and turned the ax on Thomas, aiming the massive blade for Thomas's neck.

9

CURSING, Shaun ran toward the giant. The hole was too tight for Thomas to duck back in before the ax fell. She pitched herself into the mountainous man. Her sudden movement threw off his aim. The heavy blade hit the wall, sending up sparks and chips of stone. Thomas squirmed back into the hole to safety.

The giant roared at her. He spun and elbowed her hard in the gut. The blow knocked her against the wall and forced the wind out of her in sharp rush. Gasping, she fell to the ground again. The hairy giant's belly shook with his laughter. He brought his ax up again. Shaun struggled to get her feet under her.

Her sword suddenly shot out of the hole. She dove for it, grabbing hold and bringing it up to block the giant's strike. The weapons collided with deafening clang. The impact nearly snapped her wrists.

She cried out as her hands went numb from the force and vibration. The ax skidded off her blade into her left bracer. It cleaved a ragged gash in the metal. The ruined bracer and ax dug into her flesh. Her sword fell from her numb grip when the giant yanked his ax back. Shaun sobbed through gritted teeth and cradled her bleeding arm with her other.

The numbness in her right arm faded into throbbing. She looked up at the Mordwellian. He laughed again, knowing he had her now. Even if she could get up fast enough, she could not pick up her sword, and he was blocking her path to the breach in the wall.

The giant raised his ax high above his head. Her pulse thundered in her ears, but she refused to close her eyes. She whispered a prayer to whatever god was listening that Sara and the others would make it to safety without her. The ax descended.

An arrow suddenly buried itself deep in the giant's throat. He dropped his heavy ax, narrowly missing his own foot when the blade slammed into the ground. He stumbled forward, gurgling and clawing at the feathered shaft as blood poured from the wound. He tripped over his ax's haft, pitching forward. Shaun managed to roll clear before he landed.

Her mouth agape, she nudged the fallen giant, but he did not move again. She looked up toward the wall to where she thought the arrow had come from, wondering if it was her mother who saved her. But whoever it had been was now gone.

She took several deep breaths to calm herself before she rose to her knees. Slowly she wrapped her fingers around the hilt of her sword. She crawled with it to the gap in the wall.

Thomas was gone and she could see neither Sara nor Myra. She pitched her sword through the breach and then slid into the hole, worming her way through with one arm. When she reached the other side, Sara and Myra came running to her.

"You need to help Thomas," Myra told her.

She pointed at Thomas several paces away, battling another Mordwellian soldier. Though the soldier was not as large as the giant, Thomas's movements were sluggish with exhaustion. The body of another Mordwellian lay nearby. Thomas had been busy.

Shaun kept her injured arm pressed to her as she sprinted toward Thomas. She tightened her grip on her sword and raised it high. She reached him just as his opponent smacked Thomas's sword away with the edge of his shield.

Thomas cried out and fell back as the soldier struck out at him again. Shaun blocked the Mordwellians's next strike and parried, knocking him back a step. Before the soldier could recover, Thomas rushed him, slamming into him with his shoulder.

The Mordwellian tripped and fell onto his back. Thomas reversed his blade and thrust it down into the Mordwellian's throat, the only part not covered in black mail. When the soldier ceased breathing and Thomas pulled his sword out, his face was tight with pain. His chest heaved as he tried to catch his breath.

Shaun let Thomas clean and resheathe his sword, then asked, "Is your hand broken?"

"I don't believe so. What about you?" He nodded at her arm and the bracer now covered in her blood.

"I will live."

Shaun took her sword belt from Sara when she and Myra rejoined them.

Sara gasped, "Shaun, your arm!"

She shook her head. "No time to worry about it now." She buckled her sword and belt around her hips again. "We need to keep moving. We should head for the river."

Thomas shook his head. "That takes us too far from the main road to Parna."

"We cannot take the main road. They'll be looking for us there. And all other routes pass over open ground. Our chances of reaching Parna across open fields are narrow at best. The Kerning River is surrounded by woods. That's our best option."

No matter which way they went, the Mordwellians would be looking for them. The woods at least afforded them with cover. Thomas finally nodded in agreement.

The four of them jogged down the slope on the eastern side of the city. Cottages and outbuildings in the pastures burned and smoldered. The firelight was all that lit their way. A preternatural darkness hid the stars and moon above.

They went from one burned-out structure to another as they ran toward the river. The Mordwellians had even burnt the trees and bushes to eliminate as much cover as they could. Shaun thanked the gods that they had not set the woods aflame as well.

Halfway down the hill, Shaun heard someone shout.

The four of them stopped and turned back. Shaun and Thomas laid their hands on their swords. But she saw no one. Whether it had been a cry for help or an order to halt, she could not tell, but apprehension surged through her.

She told the others, "Keep going."

They continued down the slope. The shout came again.

Shaun pointed to the smoldering remains of an outbuilding. "We'll take cover there until they are gone."

Sara touched her hand as they crouched behind the low remains of a wall. "What if they need help?"

Shaun said nothing.

The shout came a third time, much closer. Shaun's pulse surged. She slid her sword from its sheath and laid it across her lap.

Thomas tapped her shoulder. He was peering over the top of the wall and gestured for her to do the same. He pointed out a figure running down the hillside—a man in billowing robes. It was too dark for her to tell if she knew him. Five individuals pursued him down the hill. He looked back and screamed again, a clear plea this time.

Myra said, "We should help him." She and Sara were now looking over the wall as well.

Shaun weighed their options. She whispered to Thomas, "They outnumber us almost three to one." Strangely though, none of his pursuers had swords drawn or appeared to be carrying a weapon of any kind.

One of the pursuers suddenly sped forward and shoved the man in the back. He tripped and cried out as he tumbled partway down the hill. The men behind him slowed to a walk. They let him try to crawl away.

When he scrambled to his feet again, another ran forward and struck him in the stomach. The man fell once more, coughing violently. The others watched. They were playing with him.

Shaun could not stand by and watch him be killed. She gripped her sword and started to rise.

Thomas grabbed her arm. *"Wait."*

The man tried to squirm away again. His attackers formed a circle around him as she had seen wolves do once, during a hunting excursion with her parents.

A sudden burst of red lightning streaked across the sky, illuminating the man and his attackers. Shaun's breath caught in her throat. His attackers' skin was dead white and so were their eyes. One of them grinned at the man, displaying a mouth full of pointed teeth, stained red. Sara clapped her hands over her own mouth to stifle a scream.

Myra whispered, "What are they?"

Shaun opened her mouth to say she did not know, but nothing came out. The circle of creatures suddenly converged and fell on the man. His terrified screams echoed down the hillside.

Sara buried her face in Shaun's shoulder and covered her ears. Shaun's blood ran cold as his screams became more urgent, changing from screams of terror to agony. The creatures tore at him with their bare hands and teeth. Within moments his cries and struggles began to weaken.

Thomas grabbed her arm again. She jumped.

"We need to leave. *Now.*"

He grabbed Myra, cowering next to him, and pulled her away from the wall. Shaun did the same with Sara. The four of them crept away from the cover of the burned building, heading toward the woods as swiftly as they dared. They kept low to avoid drawing the creatures' attention.

The man's screams suddenly ceased altogether.

A short, high-pitched sound, almost like a whistle, cut the silence. The sound raised the hair on the back of Shaun's neck. She paused and turned to look back up the hill.

One of the creatures stood apart from the rest. It tilted its head skyward as if to sniff at the air. The image of a hunting wolf came to her mind again. Then it looked down the hill. Directly at her.

A bolt of primal fear shot through her. "No, no, no."

The others stopped and turned to look up the hill

with her. The pack broke into a run down the hillside.

Shaun spun back. "Godsdammit all, run! Don't stop!"

She grabbed Sara's hand and sprinted for the treeline. They crashed through the brush into the thick of the woods. The strange darkness thankfully did not reach there. Pale moonlight filtered down through shifting clouds and branches above as they ran. Shaun heard the creatures crash through the brush behind them, coming at a dead sprint.

She led Sara and the others deeper into the woods, hoping the creatures would give up. But the farther they went, the more treacherous the terrain was.

Branches snagged at their clothes and tree roots grabbed at their feet. Then the moonlight faded to nothing more than a dim light, the branches above too close together for the light to break through. If she did not know better, she might have thought the forest was on the side of the creatures chasing them.

She pressed ahead, blindly at times. A voice inside told her they had to slow down, but she ignored it as her breathing and the others' became ragged with fatigue. The creatures behind them showed no signs of tiring from their pursuit.

Then Myra tripped and fell. She barely managed to muffle her cry. Thomas and Shaun helped her up, but when Myra put her weight on her right leg, she bit her lip and shook her head.

"I cannot walk." Her eyes were wide with fear. She kept looking at the woods behind them.

Shaun cursed under her breath, also looking over her shoulder. The creatures were close. "Thomas, you must carry her."

Thomas knelt down, so Myra could climb onto his back.

Shaun told him, "You go on. All of you. I'll stay behind to slow the creatures down and give you more time."

"No," Sara said. "You made a promise to protect me."

"That's what I'm doing."

Sara took her hand and pleaded, "No. Not like this." Her eyes were as wide as Myra's now.

Shaun set her jaw, unwilling to let Sara see the fear she also felt. "I promised your father I would give my life to get you safely away. I have no intention of dying in these woods, but if I must give my life in order for you to escape these things, I will.

"Shaun."

"No. Go now. Please. While you can."

Thomas pulled Sara away. "We have to go, princess."

Shaun turned away, unable to meet Sara's eyes again. She expected Shaun to die. Shaun could not say she was wrong.

With only one good arm now, her chances of survival were slim. She pushed that thought aside. Swallowing hard, she wrapped both hands around the hilt of her sword as tight as she could to stop their shaking and pressed her back against a tree.

She took a deep breath and waited.

10

SHAUN heard the creatures crashing through the woods. Her eyes darted back and forth, searching for them in the dark. She wondered if they would rush her all at once or come one at a time, battering at her until she was too tired to fight them while they tore her to shreds. Neither prospect comforted her.

She wished her father was there now. He lived through the Nine Years' War, yet he never told her of any such fiends being in the Mordwellians' arsenal. What in the nine hells were they?

One of the creatures broke through the trees ahead of her. Shaun screamed as it charged her, its hands curled like claws, mouth open in a hungry grin. She lashed out with her sword but stumbled back when she got a closer look at the creature and its white eyes. They seemed to glow even in the dim moonlight.

Her hesitation cost her. The creature knocked her sword blade aside and tried to wrap her in a bear hug, its teeth going for her throat. Shaun let herself drop as a dead weight before it could get a tight grip on her. It lost its hold on her, and she landed on her knees. She dove and rolled, twisting back in the creature's direction when she came to her feet again.

It lunged at her once more, but she skipped backward, swinging for its throat. Her sword's tip cut deep into the fiend's pale flesh. Blood spurted from its neck, but the wound did not slow it down.

Shaun sidestepped its lunge, spinning as it passed her, and delivered a sweeping blow to the back of the creature's legs. The blade buried itself in the back of one. The injured leg crumpled. Still, the devil scuttled forward on its arms, trying to get to Shaun. She jumped onto its back and plunged her sword down through the back of its head with all her might. Blood sprayed her arms. The creature spasmed and went limp.

She rose to her feet again, sword at the ready. She searched the woods around her for the other creatures. There had been five. Where were the others?

No movement caught her eye, but neither could she see far into the woods, even with the dim moonlight above. Everything had gone strangely quiet. The whisper of the nearby river was the only sound that reached her. The hairs on the back of her neck, however, told her that she was still not alone.

The pale devils were watching her. The first one had been just a test.

Shaun swallowed back a tremor of fear. Better not to wait. She ran off in the direction she thought the others had gone. The fight with the creature turned her around and confused her sense of direction. She let the sounds of the river guide her forward.

The woods abruptly broke off at a rocky incline. The Kerning River rushed along below the steep edge several paces in front of her. She slowed to a walk. The moonlight was brighter here, and she could look for signs of the others. But she saw no tracks on the rocky ground.

She rubbed her forehead, considering her options. She finally turned downriver, east in the direction of Parna, and jogged farther up the incline.

Another creature exploded out of the tree line and then another. Shaun spun toward the first and beheaded it. The second creature rushed her head-on. She thrust her blade through its middle, but that did not stop it.

The creature tackled her. She fell on her back with the snarling creature on top of her. Her sword arm and the hilt of her sword were wedged between her and the creature, jabbing into her chainmail-covered chest. The fiend's white eyes stared into Shaun's as it struggled against her sword, showing no emotion, just hunger.

It gnashed its teeth and wheezed out a cold, fetid breath in her face. The creature stank of blood, the blood of the man it killed on the hillside.

She gritted her teeth as she forced her injured left arm under the creature's chin to keep it from biting her face. It dug its fingers into her ribs as if to try to pull them out with its bare hands. Her mail shirt stopped it, but a strange cold seeped through the mesh from the devil's fingers. She cried out from the cold and the painful pressure in her sides, on top of her chest, and her arms.

This only seemed to delight the creature more. It pressed down on her harder. Getting air became a struggle. The weight of the creature against her own sword crushed down on her chest. Her injured arm under the creature's chin shook with fatigue and then gave out.

The creature bit her ruined bracer as her arm fell across her face, shielding her. Foiled, it let go of her sides and grabbed her arm to pull it away from her face. Her desperate cry as she still tried to fight it was suddenly drowned out by the shriek of another of the pale fiends. It scrabbled up the rocky incline toward them.

This is how I will die—devoured by the demons of Mordwell.

The second creature pounced on her and the one on top of her. It knocked the impaled creature to the side, partially freeing her. She gasped air back into her chest. The two creatures tore at her, scratching her neck and arms.

She twisted between them with renewed strength and managed to get her sword arm free. Screaming, she battered at the creatures. She broke the impaled creature's grip and smashed her fist into the face of the other, stunning it just long enough for her to squirm free of the tangle.

Half-scrambling, half-crawling, Shaun struggled to put distance between her and the creatures. But a hand shot out and grabbed her ankle, pulling her to the ground again. She flipped onto her back. The creature gripped her leg, wrapping its cold fingers around it, and bit her. Its teeth broke through her leggings, just above her boot top, and dug into her calf.

She screamed and kicked it in the head with her free leg. The devil squealed angrily and grabbed her other leg, pulling her back toward it and the other creature again. The other was struggling to get up, but her sword through its middle hampered its efforts.

Shaun fought against the creature holding her legs. Twisting, she freed the dagger strapped to her boot and slammed it into the side of the creature's head, impaling it through the ear. The creature went limp and fell forward on her legs.

The other fiend howled as it got to its feet again. It had not bothered to pull her sword out.

Shaun kicked herself free of the dead creature. She dove forward to meet the impaled one rushing at her. Her fingers wrapped her around her sword's hilt and she rolled backwards. As she rolled, she put both boots into the creature's stomach, throwing it over her and freeing her sword.

The creature slammed to the ground. She spun to face it, letting out a howl of her own, and raised her sword high above her head. The blade came down on the creature's pale face, cleaving it in two. The dying fiend spasmed, then went still.

The sudden silence felt deafening.

Shaun staggered back, coughing. She only made it two paces before she collapsed to her hands and knees. Her chest hitched as she coughed and choked back her sobs. Her whole body shook as she fought for control.

A hand grabbed her shoulder from behind.

Shaun spun around, swinging blindly.

Thomas shouted her name as he jumped backward out of her path. "Stop!"

She stared at him. "Thomas?"

He stepped toward her. "Are you—"

She backed away from him. "*Don't*. Don't sneak up on me! Not here. Not now." She sat on the rocky ground.

"I'm sorry." He looked around at the dead creatures. "We need to go before the others find us."

Her hands still shook as she wiped her face. "There were only five. I killed four."

"And I don't want to wait to see if more of them

come looking for us. Come on. We need to go."

Shaun shouted, "*Gods above*, I need a moment!"

He frowned but said nothing else.

She closed her eyes and listened to the river. Calmer, she whispered, "I killed a man. Soldiers. Devils from some Mordwellian nightmare." She paused. "I almost died. Twice."

"I know."

"I need a moment."

Thomas crouched in front of her, putting his hands on her knees. This time she did not back away. She appreciated his human warmth after the unreal cold of the creatures.

He said quietly, "I know. But we don't have it."

She met his eyes. "I don't know what I'm doing."

"Neither do I." He sighed. "We weren't prepped for this, but we have a job to do. You are the best fighter I know. We need you. None of us will make it if you give up now."

She said nothing. He was right. She could not give up. Sara's survival depended on her.

"You are injured and tired. Come with me. I found shelter, where we can rest for the night without fear. Sara and Myra are waiting for us."

Shaun took a deep breath and allowed him to give her a hand up. She picked up her sword again and limped over to retrieve her dagger. The place where the creature bit her suddenly burned and ached at the same time.

She examined her sword and dagger in the moonlight. Both blades were a mess of dried blood and her sword blade was lined with scratches from the giant's ax blade. It would need sharpened and cleaned. She slid it back into its sheath for now.

Thomas led her up the incline to a narrow gap in the top of the rocky cliff. "There's a cave below the surface of the cliff."

"I thought you didn't like small spaces."

He nodded at the woods. "I like being hunted by those things even less."

She could not argue with that.

II

THOMAS warned her, "Watch for the rainwater pool just below the cave entrance."

He helped her slip through the gap in the clifftop. When she landed, she did so in near pitch darkness.

"Shaun!"

"Sara?"

Shaun's eyes slowly adjusted to the darkness. A low, narrow cave resolved around her. The pool that Thomas warned her of was just to the side of her. Sara and Myra sat on the other end, next to Thomas's lightstone, its brightness muffled by a square of cloth.

Sara left Myra's side. She wrapped her arms around Shaun. But Shaun winced and pulled away. She mumbled an apology.

Concern furrowed Sara's brow. "Oh! No, I am sorry. I forgot about your injuries."

"It's alright." Shaun bent forward, wincing again. Everything suddenly hurt at once.

"Here." Sara took Shaun's uninjured arm and guided her to the pool. "Sit down. Let's get your wounds cleaned."

Shaun unbuckled her sword belt and sat down, setting her sword beside her. Sara got the lightstone from Myra and set it on the cave floor next to Shaun. She unbuckled the bracer on Shaun's sword arm first.

"I need to take off the other one, but I don't want to hurt you."

Sara met Shaun's eyes. Shaun saw the worry in her eyes, but also something underneath it. Something she could not read.

She shook herself. "I can do it."

However, her hands trembled too badly for her to grip the straps and release them. She took a deep breath and closed her eyes, balling her hands into fists to steady them.

Sara put her hands on hers. "Stop. I'll undo the bindings."

Shaun looked at her again. Sara's jaw had an angry set to it, though Shaun could not understand why. She whispered, "Please don't be angry. I cannot take any more fighting tonight."

Sara's expression turned to surprise. She bowed her head and shook it. "I am not angry with you. It's everything that has happened. It's all the suffering we saw tonight and—."

She paused and put a smile on her face that Shaun could see was forced even in the cave's dimness. She was hiding something.

"Let's not talk of that now. We need to take care of your wounds."

Shaun forced a smile onto her face in kind, nodding.

Sara unbuckled the ruined bracer and eased it away from Shaun's arm. Its removal opened the tender wound again. Shaun sucked in air through her teeth and clamped her hand into a fist.

A cold sweat suddenly coated her forehead. She closed her eyes, her head bowed.

"Shaun?" The worried tone returned to Sara's voice.

Thomas murmured next to Sara, "That's bad."

"I'm fine."

Shaun forced her eyes open. The wound on her arm gaped and bled on the cave floor and Sara's hands.

Thomas went to the back of the cave. "I found something that will clean that out."

He returned and held up a small water skin. "I think this cave has been used by trappers. There were some moldy animal skins in the corner. The spring rains must flood the cave."

He cupped water from the cave pool in his hands and let it rinse over her exposed wound. Even icy cold, the water burned like fire. Shaun could not keep back her pained cry.

"Hold on," Thomas said, uncorking the water skin. "The trappers left this behind."

The smell of strong liquor struck her nose. He poured it on the wound, turning the fire into an inferno.

Shaun bit her other arm to muffle her screams. Sara held on to her as Thomas bound the wound tightly with strips of green silk from Sara's dress. The ribbons that once held back Sara's hair secured the makeshift bandages.

When he finished, Shaun murmured through a haze of pain, "I hope there's more in that water skin."

"Why?"

Shaun reached down to untie the rawhide laces on her left boot. She slipped it off and pulled her leggings up to show where the creature bit her. The round teeth marks were an angry red.

Sara exclaimed, "Gods above, Shaun! The wound looks infected." She looked at Thomas. "Could their bites be poisonous?"

"I do not know. But we should clean this right away."

Washing the bite wound with the cave water did not hurt as much as the ax wound, but when Thomas poured the last of the liquor on it, a sick sensation passed over her. She groaned, clamping her jaw shut. She refused to vomit in front of Sara and the others. Sara rubbed her shoulders.

Shaun shivered as Thomas finished wrapping the wound on her leg. The cave air suddenly felt icier than before.

He looked up from tying the last ribbon and said, "Most of the skins left behind are moldy. But there are a couple that aren't too bad."

She shook her head. "I'll be alright."

Thomas and Sara helped her limp to the other side of the cave. Holding onto the wall, she eased herself down again and looked over at Myra nearby. She had curled up under one of the skins and dozed off. Thomas left Shaun and Sara and sat next to Myra.

"We should get this mail shirt off you," Sara said softly as Shaun removed her other boot. "It cannot be very comfortable."

Shaun nodded and slowly pulled it over her head, wincing from the bruises on her chest. Sara helped her slip it over the bandages on her arm, soaked red in parts from where her blood had seeped through.

Sara left her to soak more strips of cloth in the pooled rainwater. Shaun let out a long breath and ran her fingers through her hair, trying to make herself look less disagreeable. Between the dirt from wrestling the creatures in the woods and the dried blood, she must look awful. She apologized when Sara settled next to her again.

"I must look terrifying right now."

Sara looked at her, the ghost of a smile playing at the corners of her mouth. She ran her fingertips across Shaun's forehead and down the side of her face, smoothing strands of hair back from Shaun's eyes. The softness in Sara's gaze and her touch both eased her discomfort and made her heart quicken strangely.

The smile came out more as Sara murmured, "You look like a knight."

She fell silent as she wiped the dirt and blood from Shaun's face and cleaned the scratches left by the creatures' nails. She finally muttered, "I wish I had my mending kit. The wound on your arm could use stitching. The cut above your eye, too."

Shaun rested her head against the cave wall and stared at Sara, marveling at the change in her, the strength. She had never suspected Sara could be as brave as she had proven to be.

Maybe Sara had been right. Maybe she did not see Sara at all.

"You've changed," she said when Sara finished tending to the last of her wounds.

"Have I?"

Shaun nodded. "You're stronger than you once were. When we were little, you always needed me to protect you from something. Muddy frogs at the pond, lightning storms—"

"Bullies like Darcy?" Sara looked down at her hands.

Shaun reached out and brushed Sara's hand with her fingers, speaking softly. "I had nothing to do with what happened at the park. Please believe that. But I am sorry for it happening, and I am sorry for the stupid things I said to you in the lecture hall. I was just angry and hurt."

"I know. I was angry, too." Sara's eyes met hers again. "So angry I couldn't think. I thought you wanted to get back at me for what happened between us last night."

"I would never try to hurt you that way."

"If I could go back . . ."

Shaun nodded. Sara did not have to finish. "I know."

A frown suddenly crossed Sara's face. "I hope Darcy made it to safety. I do not wish her any harm by Mordwell."

She shuddered and settled against the wall next to Shaun, pulling Shaun's arm around her shoulders. Sara laid her head against her.

"Why do you think Mordwell broke the treaty now, after so long? What happened to the House of Mackritae?"

Shaun shook her head. "I do not know."

The accord between Mordwell and Riverend had never been perfect. Mordwell had tested its bounds often, but for the most part, it held and kept the peace between the ten kingdoms intact. But something had changed. Fear wrapped itself around Shaun's gut as she wondered what that meant for Riverend and the rest of Decathea.

"Tell me everything will be alright, Shaun. I know nothing will be the same, but tell me we'll be alright and we'll defeat Mordwell again. Even if you do not believe it."

"I do believe we'll defeat Mordwell."

Though Shaun tried, she could not shake the feeling that the worst was still to come. But for Sara, for this one night, she lied.

"We'll be alright."

12

NIGHTMARES plagued Shaun. In each one, she was chased by something she could never quite see. It wheezed and snarled behind her, always one step closer. Then something touched her arm. Her eyes shot open and she sat bolt upright.

Only dim light and shadows greeted her eyes. Her hand fumbled over the cold, hard surface on which she sat. In a panic, she searched for her sword, her dagger, any weapon at all. But her boots were missing and nothing was within reach but something furry to the touch.

Thomas knelt next to her as her eyes finally adjusted and she could see the cave clearly. He handed her sword to her.

"Relax. You're safe."

She nodded, rubbing at her gritty eyes as she waited for her pulse to return to normal. The night before slowly came back to her. Her eyes trailed over the cave. Pale daylight had replaced the moonlight streaming down from the hole above. Sara sat next to Myra not far away. The two of them talked quietly.

Shaun coughed. "I need water."

Thomas passed her the water skin. "I filled it."

She tipped it back, letting the cool water soothe

her dry throat. She expected it to taste stale and full of minerals from the cave, but it did not. When she finished, she said, "This tastes fresh."

"I went down to the river to fill it this morning."

"What? *Alone?*"

"I needed to scout around so that we knew what was waiting for us outside. I figured that some fresh water wasn't a bad idea either."

Shaun frowned. "I should have gone with you."

"You needed the sleep. You're injured and slept restlessly last night. I made a judgment call. You would have decided the same if our roles were reversed."

She sighed, knowing he was probably right. "Even so, you should have awakened me sooner."

"You do us no good exhausted." His brow furrowed when she suddenly shivered. "Are you cold?"

She nodded. "It's chilly down here."

"I'm comfortable. It's much warmer outside that it was last night."

Strange. It felt no warmer to her.

Shaun heard Sara shush Myra and looked over again. Sara had her arms around Myra and stroked her hair while Myra cried. Shaun looked away, not wanting to intrude on the sorrow and fear she must feel for her family. She understood how Myra felt. She knew not what had become of her parents either.

She asked Thomas, "What do you make of what has happened? What do you think prompted this attack by Mordwell?"

Thomas shook his head. He also glanced at Myra. "I am as baffled as you. They have always tested our defenses at the border. But a siege? It's a large shift from skirmishes and abductions."

"What of those creatures? I've never heard of such things."

"Neither have I. My father was stationed for a time near Ris, by the pass through the Golden Peaks. He said he witnessed many strange things, but he never mentioned anything like those creatures. I only know that I hope not to encounter any more of them."

Another tremor passed through her. She rubbed her leg where the creature bit her. "Perhaps they belong to new rulers of Mordwell. Whoever they are."

Thomas shrugged. "Perhaps. My grandfather used to say Mordwell's sorcerers knew no bounds. Perhaps this is their doing."

With Thomas's help, she rose to her feet. "Did you find evidence of anyone else having come through the woods after us? A search party?"

"It's hard to say with the rocky terrain around the cave. I found boot and horse tracks near the river bank, though, so someone was searching there last night." He paused. "And the creatures' bodies are gone."

She frowned. "We need to get away from here. I think we should cross the river, put it between us and anyone— or *anything*—that is looking for us. What is the state of Myra's ankle?"

"She can stand, but walking is still difficult."

Shaun wished she had thought to secure horses rather than fleeing the city on foot. Walking to Parna would take them twice as long with Myra's injury.

Thomas seemed to read her thoughts. "We can carry her still, but horses would have helped."

Shaun nodded. Thomas helped her put the mail shirt

back on and strap the bracer on her sword arm. She left the ruined one behind and strapped her sword belt around her hips.

Sara and Myra looked up when Shaun and Thomas approached them. Myra's eyes were red from crying.

Thomas said gently, "We have to go."

Myra nodded and Sara helped her to her feet.

Sara asked, "What is our plan?" Again, she sounded stronger and more confident than the young princess Shaun thought she knew.

Shaun replied, "We cross the river and keep it between us and anyone who may be following us. Then we track the Kerning's course as far as we can to Parna. Thomas and I will take turns carrying Myra."

Myra frowned. "I will only slow you down."

Shaun said, "The going will be slow either way. We'll just have to make do." She saw no reason to make Myra feel worse about her injury than she already did.

Thomas pulled himself up and out of the low cave entrance. She saw him look around to confirm they were still alone, then he turned back and reached down. Shaun helped lift Myra so that he could pull her out and then Sara.

He helped Shaun out last. A sunny day and clear blue sky greeted her when she emerged from the cave. It felt wrong to her now, as though the day should be gray and stormy instead. Sadness touched her for a moment when she realized that under different circumstances, she and Sara might have spent the day in their favorite park.

She pushed her sadness aside as Thomas knelt down for Myra, letting her climb onto his back. Then the four of them shuffled down the rocky incline toward the Kerning's banks.

Sara said to her, "You were not planning for us to swim across, I trust."

Shaun and Thomas looked at each other. They had indeed.

Reading their faces, she added, "Perhaps you two can navigate the Kerning, but Myra and I cannot. Especially not after the rains we had less than a week ago."

They descended to the river's edge and watched the wide, black waters of the Kerning rush past. The rains had swollen the river to several hands above its normal height. Even if all four of them were at full strength, Shaun wondered if they could have made it all the way across.

She shook her head. "We cannot cross here."

Thomas grunted. "Arch Bridge. It's downstream. As long as the Mordwellians have no guards there, we can cross."

It was unlikely it would be unguarded, but they had no other choice than to cross there, if they were to cross the river at all.

Shaun nodded. "We'll have to find out."

13

CROUCHED in the brush, Shaun rubbed at the bandages under her leggings while she waited for Thomas to return. A strange itching ache where she was bitten had been bothering her since late morning. The itching had come on far faster than was normal for a mere infection. She wondered if Sara was right that the creature's bite was somehow poisonous.

Shaun forced herself to stop rubbing at the bandages and looked over at Sara and Myra. They both stared through the trees in the direction of Arch Bridge. The spot where they had chosen to wait while Thomas scouted ahead was close enough to the stone bridge that Shaun could pick out a corner of it through the trees. But nothing else.

Sara turned to her. "Thomas has been gone too long."

Shaun looked up at the sun peeking through the branches overhead. Sara was right. She whispered back, "We'll give him until a count of twenty."

Her fingers tapped against the toe of one of her boots. If he did not return by then, she would be forced to leave Sara and Myra behind to go after him. That would be just another delay.

She rubbed at her forehead and the growing tension there. Her eyes slipped closed and she took a deep breath.

She held in the clean smells of soil, cedar trees, and the nearby river. They only soothed her so much.

Their pace had been slow the moment they set out from the cave. Myra was slowing them down and the group had to stop from time to time for Shaun or Thomas to scout ahead for threats. If whatever was wrong with Shaun's own leg got worse, they might not reach Parna by the next day. The day they were to reunite with the king.

If they could not make it in time, would the king wait? Or would they be forced to find refuge in Parna until someone sent for them? The idea of waiting in Parna while gods-knew-what happened back in Riverend left her with anxious knots inside.

Sara broke through her thoughts. "*Shaun!* Someone is coming."

Shaun drew her sword as silently as she could manage. Thomas emerged from the brush a few paces ahead.

She glared at him. "What took you so long?"

The frown on Thomas's face said he did not have good news. "We have company."

"More creatures?"

"No. They appear to be regular soldiers."

"How many?"

"I saw two guarding the bridge, but there may be more I couldn't see. And getting close enough to ambush them will be a problem. There are no cover trees close to the bridge. Everything has been clear cut on this side."

Shaun's frown matched his.

Thomas went on, "However, I think we must try to take them—there is a covered wagon parked by the side of the bridge." His mouth curled in a small, hopeful smile.

Sara gasped. "That would be a great fortune if we

could use it, but is it unoccupied? I won't steal someone's trailer, just to reach Parna faster."

Thomas shrugged. "I saw no driver. No one besides the two Mordwellians."

"Maybe the driver was captured," Myra suggested. "If so, we can free him and try to persuade him to take us to Parna."

Shaun nodded. They needed that wagon, driver or not. "Then it's agreed."

Thomas said, "You and I can take to the river. We'll approach the bridge from the water, then climb ashore and ambush them from behind."

"That sounds like our best bet. The current should be manageable if we stay in the shallows." She told Sara, "You and Myra stay here. Keep hidden, and we'll return for you."

Sara frowned. "I am not fond of this plan."

Shaun did not love it either, but saw no other way. "We have precious few options. The longer we're out here, the longer you are in harm's way."

She took off her mail shirt and handed her sword to Sara. "Use it to defend yourself if you need to."

Sara took it, her eyes wide. "What about you? You need your sword and your armor."

"They will only weigh me down in the water."

Thomas handed his own mail shirt and sword to Myra.

Sara pulled Shaun into a sudden embrace. "Make sure you come back." She looked Shaun in the eye when she pulled away. "*Both* of you. We all must reach Parna, not just Myra and I."

Shaun squeezed Sara's hand before she ducked into the thick brush, following Thomas to the river bank.

They paused to watch the swift black waters and then waded in. The current tugged at Shaun's legs, even in the shallows. When the water reached to her waist, she sank down and let herself float into the current. It snatched her up and swept her downstream with a speed that made her heart leap into her throat.

Arch Bridge came into view within moments. She paddled against the current to slow herself, but it had little effect. Thomas swam ahead of her and steered himself toward one of the bridge's stone and wood supports. He just managed to catch hold and stop himself. He reached out his hand for Shaun.

Her momentum almost yanked Thomas loose from the bridge support when she grabbed his hand. His face pinched in a grimace and he hugged the support tighter, slowly pulling Shaun toward him. When it was within her reach, she grabbed onto the support to pull herself closer. The current continued to tug at them as it rushed past, trying to pull them off the support.

Thomas murmured, "Let's wait here for a moment." His breathing came fast and he shuddered.

Shaun agreed, even though the coolness of the water was making her fingers go numb.

"Alright," he finally said. "Take my hand and we'll swim together for the bank."

They kicked off from the bridge support. The current hungrily tugged at them, trying to yank them off course. She suddenly wished she had kept her mail shirt, anything to give her more weight and resistance against the river. She and Thomas paddled as hard as they could and still keep from alerting the soldiers with the noise.

As soon as Shaun felt the rocky bank under her, she

dug her boots in and dove for the exposed shore. On dry land, Shaun and Thomas huddled together and shivered.

The scrape of boots on the stone surface of the bridge came to Shaun from above. A soldier said something in a strange, guttural language that she guessed to be Mordwellian. The other soldier grunted and responded in the same foreign tongue.

Shaun gestured at Thomas to indicate she would go to the edge of the bridge for a better look. She crept along the underside of the bridge and peered out at their targets. One of the soldiers stood off to the side of the bridge, his back to her. From where she crouched, she could also see the covered wagon Thomas told them about.

Decorated with red, blue, and gold paint, it was hard to miss, even tucked into a nearby stand of trees. A small house-like structure with a peaked roof, windows, and a door at one end sat atop the wagon base. It looked large enough for only two people, but the wide driver's bench would accommodate both her and Thomas, while Sara and Myra rode in the back.

However, she could not see a horse to go with the wagon. Shaun prayed the Mordwellians had not killed it. She cared less what might have happened to the trailer's owner. A trailer with no horse would be as much good to them now as a boat with no oars.

She slipped back under the cover of the bridge. Turning to Thomas, she pointed to his side of the bridge and then her side and raised three fingers. He nodded and moved to the opposite edge of the bridge, slipping his dagger from its sheath on his belt. Shaun drew hers as well.

They each held a hand up and counted down from three, then rounded the bridge in unison. Shaun kept low and darted up the river bank, staying behind the Mordwellian, who still had his back turned to her.

The sun behind her made her shadow too long to keep her hidden. The soldier dropped his hand to his sword and turned. Before he could draw it, Shaun jammed her dagger into his leather-armored ribs as hard as she could and clamped her arm around his neck to keep him from pulling away. He screamed in agony and struggled to get free from her. Shaun held fast until his knees buckled. She let his body drop, pulling her dagger free as he fell.

She turned toward Thomas. He outmatched the other man in both height and frame, but his dagger put him at a disadvantage against the soldier's sword. Metal sang out as he fended off the soldier's swipes with rapid strikes.

The soldier growled and thrust his sword at Thomas's middle. Thomas danced to the side and slashed the soldier's arm, throwing the other man off-balance. Spinning around behind him, Thomas grabbed the soldier around the neck, pulled him in, and plunged his dagger into the Mordwellian's chest. The soldier's eyes rolled back as he fell.

Shaun saw no one else on the bridge or near the wagon. She let her dagger hand fall to her side as she turned to Thomas. "That was easier than I thought it would be."

Thomas nodded and pulled his dagger free from the dead soldier's chest. As he turned back to her, a low groan came from the wooden steps at the back of the wagon behind her. Thomas's eyes went wide.

"Duck!"

Something *whooshed* overhead just as Shaun ducked

her head and shoulders. She caught the glint of sunlight off metal as she spun toward whoever attacked her. An armored elbow connected with Shaun's cheekbone. Bright stars flashed in her vision, blocking out everything else.

14

EVERYTHING tilted crazily as Shaun fell to her hands and knees on the sandy ground. She tasted the metallic tang of blood. Eyes shut, Shaun shook her head, trying to clear it.

Nearby, Thomas shouted, followed by a scuffling of feet. Shaun opened her eyes just as Thomas ducked under a morning star swung by a bald, wiry-limbed albino. Scale mail covered the albino's arms from wrist to elbow.

Thomas's lack of a weapon other than his dagger put him at a disadvantage to the albino's long limbs and the morning star's reach. The albino's attacks forced him to dodge more than strike. His chest heaved with ragged breaths.

The albino grinned and swung two-handed. Thomas tried to jump back, but stumbled. The morning star's spikes ripped through Thomas's tunic and sliced into his arm and shoulder. He cried out as he fell.

"Thomas!"

Shaun picked herself up and dove, shoulder first, into the albino's exposed side. The impact knocked him down, but she tripped over his flailing legs. Without thinking, she put her injured arm down to stop her fall. Pain shot up her arm.

A sudden rush of blood poured down her hand as the bindings on her forearm stretched and tore. Shaun gritted her teeth and tucked her arm against her chest. She got her feet back under her at the same time as the albino. He struck out at her, forcing her back.

Thomas grunted and threw his dagger at the albino. It buried itself in the Mordwellian's shoulder. He roared and dropped the morning star. Glaring at Thomas, he grabbed for the dagger's hilt.

Shaun took advantage of his distraction and slammed her foot into the side of his leg. His knee gave way with a sickening crack. Agony pinched the albino's face. He opened his mouth wide and let loose a high-pitched scream. Shaun recoiled in horror as he crumpled to the ground.

The albino had no tongue.

Thomas charged him, wielding one of the dead Mordwellians' swords. He plunged it through the prone man's throat. Blood spewed from the wound, spraying Thomas. The albino made only a short gasp before his body went limp.

Falling back, Thomas took a moment to catch his breath before he looked at her. "Don't say 'that was too easy' ever again."

Turning away after a nod of agreement, she spat out the blood in her mouth. Her fingers searched for the tooth that was knocked loose when the albino struck her. She grabbed hold of it and yanked it out with a muffled scream.

Cursing, she went to the river bank and rinsed her mouth with river water. Even its coolness did not keep the water from stinging.

She returned to Thomas to examine his wounds. Blood had soaked partway down his tunic. The wounds would need bandaged as soon as they found something to bind them with. If they could find needle and thread, a few of the cuts could use some stitching.

She asked, "Can you still move your arm?"

He nodded and leaned on her to stand up. "I think I got lucky. The cuts mostly just hurt like hell. What about you? You don't look any better than me."

Shaun looked down at her arm. Blood had soaked through the bandages. "Other than the good tooth I lost, I'll be fine. We need to get your wounds cleaned and find the horse that belongs to this wagon before someone comes back to check on these three." She nodded at the dead Mordwellians.

"Agreed."

After they cleaned Thomas's wounds, they examined the state of the abandoned wagon. Given the broken bindings at the front, it appeared as though the horse had broken free on its own. The rest of the rig looked fine. The driver, however, was in no shape to answer questions about which way the horse might have gone. They found his corpse inside the small house on wheels.

Just as his horse was missing, so was his head. Shaun stared down at the man's neck, or the bloody stump that used to be his neck. It appeared it had been twisted until someone ripped his head clean off. She wondered what it would take for someone to do that. Surely, no one human.

Her hand went to her throat. "What do you think did that to him?"

Thomas shook his head. "I don't know, and I don't want to stick around to find out."

Judging from the lack of blood inside the wagon, he had been killed elsewhere before his body was deposited inside. But why discard the head, only to keep the body? Or was it the other way around?

Shaun swallowed and nodded. "We better get him out of here. We don't want Sara and Myra seeing this."

The man obviously had not been tall—his gold velvet pants would have been too short on her—but he was quite broad in the shoulders and round in the middle. Subduing him would have been no easy task. Carrying him out would be just as hard.

Thomas made a sour face. "I'll take his shoulders. You take his feet."

Shaun grabbed the corpse's ankles. They both grunted as they lifted. Their burden's heft forced them to half carry, half drag it into the woods. Shaun wished they could give the man a proper burial, but there was no time.

They left the dead man where no one could see him from the road and gave him a silent prayer before they set off after the horse. Shaun prayed he and the gods forgave them.

Thomas found hoof tracks leading into the woods in the opposite direction from where Sara and Myra waited. Shaun frowned, knowing they had no choice but to follow where the tracks led. She and Thomas set off at a jog. They stopped every so often to whistle, hoping the horse would come to them.

The bite wound on Shaun's leg started to ache after a time. She forced herself to keep going, cursing herself for not being able to fight the creature off before it bit her. But the ache finally got bad enough that she could not ignore it. She came to a limping stop.

Thomas jogged a few more paces, then stopped as well. She bent over to cover her wincing.

When he returned to her side, Thomas asked, "Are you alright?"

Shaun nodded. "I just need to rest a moment."

She cleared her throat and knelt down to tie her boot tighter. Brief pain stabbed her ankle, then faded back to a manageable level. But when she stood, a wave of dizziness struck her. She closed her eyes, swaying on her feet.

Thomas grabbed her shoulder. "Shaun?"

She opened her eyes, shaking her head. "I'm fine. I just stood up too fast."

Worry lines crisscrossed his forehead. "You do not look well."

Shaun wiped sweat from her forehead. A sudden chill made her shudder. "I am just tired and hungry."

He nodded, but said nothing.

"Come on. We don't want the horse to get too far ahead." Without waiting, she set off again, this time at a walk.

Thomas sighed behind her. He jogged to catch up.

"It's probably the blood loss." He gestured at the bloody bandages on her forearm. "I feel a little lightheaded myself."

Shaun nodded and whistled for the horse. Still nothing. She sighed and rubbed at her damp forehead again.

After a time, Thomas said, "I think you should tell Sara."

Shaun glanced at him. "Tell her what?"

Thomas kept his eyes on the woods. "How you feel. In case something happens and we don't get out of this alive, she should know."

She stared at him. "How I feel about what?"

He looked over at her and raised an eyebrow. "How you feel about her."

Shaun stopped walking.

Thomas stopped as well, turning back.

Her brow came down in a glare and she rested her hands on her sides. "What are you talking about?" Her heart suddenly pounded in her chest.

Thomas rolled his eyes. "I saw how you two were last night. It's pretty obvious."

Shaun blinked, wondering if Thomas thought he was being funny. If he was, she would have to reconsider their friendship. There was nothing funny about what he was suggesting.

He went on. "There's nothing wrong with admitting it. She might feel the same way. But you won't know unless you tell her first."

Shaun crossed her arms as her mind raced through ways to explain away whatever he thought he saw. She shook her head, settling on simple denial. Through numb lips, she said, "I don't know what you're talking about."

Thomas threw his hands up. "Sure you don't. The way you look at her sometimes? Like last night. I don't look at my friends that way.

"Then there's the petty fights that keep happening with you two. The way you talk endlessly about her when you're fighting. When I have an argument with one of my friends, I don't worry about it half as much as you do when you're fighting with her. Gods forbid Sara gives you the silent treatment. I sometimes think you might explode."

He paused to let his words sink in. "And why do you think that is?"

She closed her eyes. Her head hurt suddenly. "Stop talking already."

"No. If you will not say it, I will. You love Sara."

Shaun's eyes shot open as her breath caught in her chest. She stalked forward. "Take it back." She shoved him in the chest, glaring at him.

He fell back a step. "Are you being serious?"

"You heard me." She pushed him again and growled, "Take it back."

He pushed her back, also glaring. "Fine! If you want to be childish about it, fine. Just pretend I'm crazy. Pretend I have no idea what I'm saying."

Shaun caught the hurt look on his face before he turned his back on her and started walking again. She stared after him, then dropped her gaze.

They had never had a fight before. Not a serious one. But Shaun could not bring herself to apologize. He had no right to accuse her of having feelings beyond friendship for Sara.

Sara was her best friend. Nothing more.

Still, Shaun could not help but think back to the night before. She had felt something in the look in Sara's eye, the way Sara touched her. Shaun swallowed and stared at the ground.

There was more than concern in Sara's eyes and her touch. Something that had not been there before. At the thought of Sara's touch, she felt another rush inside.

She bit her lip and looked after Thomas. What if he was right? That would change too many things for her to count, including her role as Sara's Watcher.

Shaking her head, she blew out a sigh and ran her fingers through her short hair. No. Thomas was not right. He could not be right.

She set off after him at a brisk pace until she caught up . Neither looked at the other as they walked.

Shaun muttered, "Let's just find that damned horse and get out of here."

15

SHAUN crept toward the brown and white speckled mare. The mare paused and raised her head from the stand of bushes where she was grazing. She regarded Shaun and snorted, twitching her tail. Shaun stopped.

She kept her voice low. "It's alright. We won't hurt you."

The mare's tail swished once more, then fell still. Shaun took another step forward, hardly daring to breathe. The mare watched Shaun, but made no other move. Shaun's hand shook as she reached out and placed her hand on the horse's speckled neck. The mare turned her head, regarding Shaun with calm brown eyes.

She ran her shaking hand over the horse's thick neck, whispering, "You're alright. I won't hurt you."

Shaun took hold of the horse's bridle. She did not shy from Shaun's touch and let Shaun lead her out of the bushes and back to the covered wagon.

Thomas took down a coil of rope from a hook on the side of the house-like structure and cut a long section from it. He tied one end to the rig's front axle, the other to the mare to keep her close.

Shaun watched him loop the rope through the horse's bridle. "We need to go back for Sara and Myra."

Thomas nodded without looking at her. "You go. I'll

work on repairing the broken harness."

"Maybe there are bandages inside for your shoulder."

"Maybe." He walked away.

Shaun sighed, hands on her hips, and turned back in the direction of where they left Sara and Myra. If that was how he wanted to be, so be it.

The itch in her leg started again, then the ache, despite the tighter laces on her boots. She paused near the hiding place where Sara and Myra should be and wiped away the thin sheen of sweat coating her forehead.

Her brow furrowed as she crouched to rub at her leg again. With the intensifying ache, she could not be sure she could still carry Myra on her back and manage to walk back to the wagon. Asking Sara to get Thomas and the horse to carry them both back was not what any of them needed either.

She stood again, slowly this time, willing herself to rise above the pain. "Sara?"

Sara and Myra stood up from the brush. Shaun picked her way through to them.

Sara gasped. "You're hurt again." She reached out to touch the bruises on Shaun's face, but Shaun dodged her hand. Sara's brow furrowed. "What's wrong?"

"Nothing." She paused. "It's nothing. I'm alright."

Sara let her hand drop. She handed back Shaun's mail shirt. "You don't look alright."

Myra asked, "What about Thomas?"

"He was wounded, but he should be fine as well." Shaun slipped the mail shirt over her head and took her sword from Sara, avoiding her eyes. "But we should hurry back. His wounds still need wrapped, and I don't trust that he can defend himself if someone comes looking for the Mordwellians we killed."

Myra nodded. "I think I can walk on my own, as long as it's not far."

Shaun allowed herself a sigh of relief. "It's not."

Sara handed Thomas's sword and armor to Shaun and offered her arm to Myra. "Lean on me for support if you need it."

Myra gave her a grateful smile.

Shaun led them back. By the time they reached the wagon, Thomas had finished repairing the bindings and was running a brush he had found over the horse's speckled coat.

Myra gasped quietly. "Oh, she's beautiful!"

Shaun left her and Sara to coo over the mare and pulled herself up into the wagon. She hoped the owner had left behind both bandages and something to cover the gaudy paint on the outside.

Her eyes trailed over the menagerie of musical instruments hanging from hooks sunk into the arched roof's beams. Masks stared down at her from one wall, next to a narrow rack stuffed with what looked like costumes, all of them as gaudy as the wagon's exterior. A small dressing table stood next to a wide bed built into the far end. The simple coverlets on the bed made it look oddly domestic next to the rest of the inside.

She opened a tall cabinet and found another jumble of items stacked inside. Pots, various foodstuffs, reams of brightly colored silk and velvet, tarot cards, bandages, a pair of wax-wrapped liquor bottles, half-unrolled scrolls. At the bottom of the cabinet, she found two lidless, empty paint pots and one with its lid still on.

Smiling, Shaun pulled out the lidded pot. It felt full in

her hand. But she groaned when she took the lid off and peered inside.

Crimson.

She thumped the pot back down on the cabinet shelf. Nothing else in the cabinet looked suitable for covering the gaudy exterior. The owner's focus seemed to have been on entertaining more than anything practical.

Running her fingers through her hair, Shaun blew out a frustrated breath. She stared into the cabinet. Nothing new appeared in it. She sighed and took two bundles of the bandages out before she shut the cabinet.

Her eyes trailed over the rest of the things in the wagon. She went to the dressing table and rooted through its drawers. Still she found nothing useful.

She started to turn away, but then her gaze fell on a corked leather pouch lying on the dressing table. Her nose wrinkled when she sniffed the contents—some liquor she could not identify, certainly not an ale or mead, the extent of her experience with such drinks. She started to set it back on the table and then stopped, staring at it. Instead, she tucked it into the back of her belt. Then she climbed out of the covered wagon.

The mare's ear turned in Shaun's direction as she approached Thomas. "There's nothing in there to cover the ridiculous paint, but I found bandages." She held one bundle up. "I saw needle and thread in the dressing table, too, if you think your wounds need stitched."

Thomas just nodded.

Myra took the bandages from Shaun. "I will help you bind your wounds, Thomas. I make no guarantees about stitching, though. I'm not sure I can stomach that."

He smiled and set the brush on the driver's bench.

Shaun turned away from them, walking down to the river. She knelt at its edge and untied the silk rags wrapped around her forearm, careful not to tug at the wound. It bled a little as the silk was pulled away.

Sara asked from behind her, "Why not let me help you?" She tucked the bottom of her dress around her and crouched next to Shaun.

She glanced at Sara. "I can wrap the wounds myself." But when she put the bandages under one arm to keep them off the wet bank, they started to slip free as soon as she reached to gather water for cleaning the wound. She blew out a frustrated sigh.

Sara held out her hand. "Will you at least allow me hold those for you?"

Shaun sighed again, but agreed.

Sara watched her in silence, then asked, "Did something happen between you and Thomas? You are both quiet, more than usual."

She shook her head, lying, "We're just tired." She glanced sidelong at Sara, but could not tell if Sara believed her. "There was an extra Mordwellian guarding the wagon that we didn't see. He's the one who wounded Thomas. It wasn't an easy kill."

"Are any of them?"

Shaun looked at her again, shaking off her wet arm. "This is what we've been trained to do."

Sara stared at her, searching her face. "Does that mean killing doesn't affect you?"

Shaun allowed herself to meet Sara's eyes, wondering what she wanted to hear. She looked away again and gave her a small shrug. "We were not trained to think about how it affects us." The answer sounded simplistic, even to her own ears.

Staring out at the river rushing past them, she added, "I've tried not to think about it much. If I did . . ." She let her words trail off.

Sara tore a piece of cloth from the bundle, then took Shaun's arm. "I understand."

Shaun let Sara dab the wound dry with the bandages, watching her. When Sara started to unroll more of the cloth, though, Shaun stopped her.

"I can do the rest." She held out her hand.

A brief look of hurt passed over Sara's face, but she handed the bandages to Shaun. "Very well." She stood up. "I'll go see if Myra needs help."

Shaun nodded, only glancing at Sara when she walked away, and set to wrapping her injured arm. She paused when she finished and looked over her shoulder to make sure Sara was with the others. As much as it hurt them both, she had to distance herself from Sara.

If Thomas thought there was something between her and Sara, then others would, too. That would cause trouble for them both, something she could not allow. She also did not want Sara to see what she was about to do next.

She unlaced and removed her boot to expose the bite wound. The silk rags around it were brown from the rubbing leather and oozing blood. The itch intensified as Shaun unbound her leg.

The wounds no longer bled, nor did they look infected. They looked to have closed already and the skin around the marks was not the angry red she expected to see. What concerned her were the three, dark red bumps just under the skin where she was bitten. She gently poked at them. They were firm to the touch. Not hard, as if there were pebbles under her skin, more like miniature peas, just barely cooked through.

Swallowing, she took out her dagger and the pouch she took from the wagon. She cleaned her dagger with the liquor inside the pouch, then positioned the dagger's point over the bumps. Gritting her teeth, she jabbed the dagger into one of them.

She had to stop when the bleeding got too bad. It obscured the wound and kept her from seeing what the bump might be. When she tried to squeeze the wound, white hot pain shot up her ankle. She clamped her jaw shut before a cry escaped her.

Tears stung her eyes as she looked over her shoulder again. Thomas was leading the speckled mare to the front of the wagon. She did not have much time. Shaun cursed and turned her attention back to the bite wounds.

As quickly as she could, she ran the dagger over each of the bumps, opening the skin. She could not bring herself to try again to squeeze out whatever poison or substance the Mordwellian devil had left behind. With shaking hands, she poured the contents of the pouch over the open wounds. She shut her eyes and pounded a fist into the sandy river bank until the pain faded.

She wrapped the last of the bandages around her leg, cinching them tight. When she put her boot back on, she left the laces looser than before to let the wounds dry. She rose and put weight on her wounded leg. It held her with less complaint than she expected.

Bending down, Shaun resheathed her dagger in its place in her other boot and picked up the nearly empty pouch. She stared at it a moment, then raised it to her lips, chugging down the last of its contents. Maybe the liquor would dull the pain enough to let her hide it a little longer.

Whatever the liquor was, it burned its way down her throat. She coughed deeply when she finished it. Before she turned back to the others, she threw the pouch into the Kerning's dark waters.

When Shaun reached the others, Thomas was still at the front of the wagon. Sara told her, "We're ready if you are."

"I am."

She helped Myra up into the house-like structure, then offered Sara a hand up. Sara turned back once she was inside.

"Will you ride with us?"

Shaun shook her head. "I should ride up front with Thomas, in case we run into more trouble."

Sara nodded. If she was disappointed, her face did not betray her. She asked, "Are you sure everything is alright with you?"

For a moment, Shaun said nothing, then, "I'll just be glad to get to Parna." She forced a smile onto her face.

Sara gave a smile in return that looked equally forced. "As will we all."

Shaun shut the door for her. A lock snapped into place inside. Thomas met her eye when Shaun climbed up to the driver's bench, but she settled next to him without a word, turning her eyes to the road ahead.

She knew she should apologize to him, but she could not bring herself to do so. He finally sighed and snapped the reins, turning the horse and its burden toward Arch Bridge and the road to Parna.

16

AN UNNATURAL quiet followed them as they rode through the remains of the day, stopping only to rest the mare. Shaun kept a vigilant eye on the hillsides and woods surrounding them. As the day wore on, a vague sickness settled into her gut. She tried to tell herself it was just nerves caused by the strange quiet around them.

The road was a main thoroughfare for merchants and other travelers, but they saw no one ahead of them and no one behind. No one had even passed them. And no one sat by the side of the road.

She considered the possibility that the Mordwellians had taken over the road at some cross point, detaining every traveler. If so, how far east or west were the Mordwellians from their position? Were they riding straight into a trap?

Shaun said none of this to Thomas. If he had similar misgivings, he kept them to himself as well. They had no choice but to stay their course, if they wanted to reach Parna by the next day, trap or no.

When the sky darkened with twilight's approach, Thomas suggested they stop for the night. Shaun hesitated. He added, "I don't think we should push through the night on an unfamiliar road."

She thought about this, then nodded. "You're probably

right." Staring off into the woods, she said, "I hope we don't find more of those creatures in these woods."

"I suppose we have no choice but to find out."

Shaun said nothing. She had begun to tire of those words: no choice.

Thomas steered the horse off the road, then slowed her to a walk. "We need to get off the road as far as we can."

He pointed the mare toward an opening between the trees. The space between them was just ample enough to admit the wide covered wagon, and the brush was just low enough that the rig would not get stuck on it. As they rode into the woods, the axles squeaked and the wagon groaned as it bumped and swayed over the uneven ground.

Shaun sat up, taking her feet down from where she had rested them on the brass bar in front of her. She grabbed hold of the handle above her, attached to the wooden overhang above the driver's bench.

Thomas let the horse pick her own way through the brush, down into a shallow hollow. He pulled her to a halt when the wagon had leveled out, fully in the depression, and eased the brake lever forward and locked it into place. Shaun climbed down from the driver's bench and followed him to help get the mare out of her bindings.

He glanced at Shaun. "The wagon should be hard to see from the road, once night falls."

She nodded.

Thomas led the mare out. "I'll get her hobbled, then scout around to make sure we're alone out here."

She turned away, heading for the back of the wagon.

Light spilled from the back of it. The door was already open. Shaun's hand fell to the hilt of her sword.

Above her, a soft glow lit the edges of the windows on the side of the structure, muted by dark curtains.

She rounded the back of the wagon. Sara smiled down at her from the open doorway, silhouetted against the light of two small lanterns inside. She gestured at the wagon's built-in cabinets.

"I think we should sit down to a proper meal tonight."

Shaun slid her hand from her sword to her belt and took a calming breath. A smile crept its way onto her face as she nodded at Sara. She had not eaten much when they stopped to rest the mare, feeling too sick to eat with the others. But a grumble came from inside her now.

"That sounds like a great idea."

Myra looked around Sara. "Can we chance building a fire? The dried meats might taste better if they are warmed. The bread we found, too."

Shaun looked toward the front of the rig. The mare had been hobbled and was nipping at something growing out of a rotted stump of a tree. Thomas was nowhere to be seen.

"Thomas went to scout around, but I doubt he'll find anyone out here. I think a small fire won't hurt."

She did not relish the idea of spending a night in the hollow with no fire. Gods knew what was out there, watching them.

She added, "It'll get rather cold tonight without one." Even with the warm temperatures of the day, this late in the summer, the nights got cold.

While Sara and Myra put together a meal, Shaun gathered what dry branches she could find close to the wagon. She had a fire started when Thomas returned. As she had hoped, he found no one in the woods.

Myra and Sara joined them at the fire. Myra handed each of them a thick splinter of wood from a branch she had broken up. Dried meat was spitted onto one point so it could be dangled near the fire to warm.

Sara looked at Shaun and the others. "I am saddened about the man who owned the wagon losing his life to the Mordwellians. Now that we are all gathered over a proper meal, I want to offer him a prayer and our hopes that he has found his way to a more peaceful place beyond this world.

"I also want to give thanks to our gods for allowing us to find his wagon so that we have a better means to reach Parna." She paused and smiled sheepishly. "And our thanks to them for the man leaving us this food . . . because I was *so* hungry when I woke this morning."

The others murmured their agreement and bowed their heads with her. Shaun prayed again for the dead man and gave thanks for the food, but more so, she prayed for expediency in their travels the next day.

The others made quiet, lighthearted conversations while they ate. Shaun nodded along with them, but heard little of what they said, preoccupied by her own troubled thoughts about the road ahead. They tumbled through her mind until Myra announced she wanted to turn in.

Sara replied, "That sounds like an excellent idea. We still have a lot farther to travel tomorrow before we reach Parna."

She looked at Shaun and Thomas. "How should we arrange sleeping in the wagon? Two of us can share the bed, and there are more blankets in the cabinet below the bed. We can make up beds on the floor of the wagon as well."

Shaun glanced at Thomas before she said, "It's alright. Thomas and I should set a watch and sleep in shifts out here."

Sara shook her head. "It will be too cold for you."

Thomas replied, "We would only wake you when one of us gets up to switch watch with the other."

Shaun nodded in agreement.

Then a drop of water fell on her head. She looked up into the sky above the hollow to see the moon's light muted behind thick clouds. The second drop struck her forehead. It was followed by another and another, until the drops became a gentle rain.

Thomas groaned. Rain water trickled over his close-cropped dark hair, down his face.

Myra held her hands over her head, giggling. "Do you want to reconsider?"

He sighed and shook his head. "We will be fine. There is plenty of room under the wagon for us to sleep there. We won't drown."

They both rose and Thomas helped Myra to the wagon. Sara watched them go, then looked at Shaun. "You haven't eaten much today."

"I was not hungry for most of it."

Sara studied her for a moment. Shaun forced herself not to look away this time.

"I smelled Panagresh brandy on you before. I recognized it, because my father was given a bottle once." Sara paused, as if expecting Shaun to deny this. "Was it from the bottles we found in the wagon?"

Shaun wondered if she could blame her sour stomach on that, at the same time as she tried to think of an explanation other than the truth. She shrugged finally. "I found a skin filled with it on the dressing table when I went looking for something to bandage Thomas's wounds. I used it on my wounds, to clean them. Maybe it got on my hands, too."

Sara's brow wrinkled. "Are your wounds infected?"

Shaun lied to her. "No, and I want to keep it that way." She paused and forced half a smile onto her face. "I am fine. Don't worry."

Sara finally nodded and stood up. "Goodnight, then. Try to get some rest."

"I will."

She watched Sara walk away and Thomas help her into the wagon. Then she turned her gaze to the fire, rubbing her hands over her face. The falling rain chilled her skin.

The brandy had eased the pain in her leg and filled her with a small warmth, fighting back the cold tremors that had been growing ever more frequent. But its warmth had faded long ago. She prayed that the brandy she poured on her leg had at least remedied whatever sickness had been growing there. She could not fall ill now.

A breeze blew across the hollow, making the flames in front of her jump and dance. A violent shiver passed through her. She wrapped her arms tightly around herself, suddenly wishing she had a cloak with her.

A blanket suddenly fell over her shoulders. Shaun turned her head to see Sara standing next to her. She had not even heard Sara approach.

She knelt down next to Shaun. "I trust you won't refuse a blanket." She raised an eyebrow. "Or would you prefer to freeze rather than admit you're cold, knight?"

Shaun allowed herself a quiet laugh. "I thank you for

your kindness, m'lady."

Sara smiled and kissed Shaun lightly on the cheek before she got up again. "Goodnight, Shaun."

"Goodnight."

Sara left her alone again. Shaun pulled the blanket tightly around herself. Thomas sat down across the fire from her, a blanket of his own in his hands. He grumbled about the rain as he unfurled it and draped it over his broad shoulders.

They sat in silence for a time. Shaun glanced at him, then sidelong toward the wagon, making sure the door was now closed. She could not keep ignoring what had happened between her and Thomas, but she could not risk Sara overhearing her either.

She told him, "You had no right to suggest I have improper feelings for Sara—*the king's daughter.*"

Thomas looked at her across the fire. "You would not be the first."

"Why would that matter? You know what it would mean for me, if something like that were true, which it's not."

She tossed the last of the dry kindling into the fire. Keeping the fire going would be a losing battle, if the rain persisted.

Thomas frowned. "Alright. I was wrong. I apologize."

She rolled her eyes. "You're just saying that. You don't really mean it."

He leaned forward, dropping his voice. "I don't want to fight with you. We have enough on our hands already without us trying to fight each other."

Shaun dropped her voice in kind. "We're not fighting. We're just talking."

Thomas glared at her. "You're like a man sometimes, you know."

Shaun blinked and recoiled a little. *"What?"*

"I suggest you have feelings for someone, and you do everything in your power to deny it. Is that not what women accuse us men of doing all the time? Shutting our hearts away?"

Shaun said nothing. Too many retorts tumbled through her mind for her to pick one. She wanted to tell Thomas it was his fault she felt so strange around Sara now. That she felt nothing for Sara other than friendship before he opened his big mouth. But she stopped herself each time she started to speak, knowing none of these things were because of him.

Thomas stared at her, but Shaun ignored him and stared down into the fire. Anger burned inside her. She closed her eyes, refusing to make Thomas her outlet for it.

She muttered, "I don't even know even know what's true anymore." It was more to herself than to him.

"Are you alright?"

Shaun opened her eyes, surprised at the question. "Why do you and Sara keep asking me that? And don't try to change the subject."

"I'm not." He paused. "You don't look well and you've been shivering."

"I'm just cold. From the rain."

He studied her. "It isn't that cold tonight, even with the rain."

She fell silent, running out of excuses. Finally she admitted, "The bite from that creature may be infected. Or poisoned."

Thomas's brow furrowed, more in irritation than

concern. "How long have you been hiding this?"

Shaun looked away. "You're going to accuse me of hiding this, too?"

"You did, though, did you not?" He sighed. "I am your friend and your fellow apprentice knight. You shouldn't have kept this from me."

"I know . . . I didn't want anyone to worry."

"You mean Sara. You didn't want *Sara* to worry."

She looked back at him. "Please stop."

The separation between Watchers and Wards was made clear to her and all others from the time they entered the Watcher program. Watchers were the protector first, friend second, more than a friend never. Normally, apprentice knights are not even allowed to be Watchers for friends. The only reason an exception had been made for her was because of Sara's insistence upon it and her father's acquiescence. He went to Knights Master Farrash and made the request himself.

If ever a romantic relationship developed between a Watcher and Ward and it was discovered, not only was the Watcher removed from the program, they could face outright dismissal from the Knights Service. The fact that Sara was a princess made such a dismissal all the more likely. The possibility shot fear straight through her heart.

Shaun met Thomas's eyes. "Even if it were true that I have feelings toward Sara, I can never act on them."

"If it is true, you need to step down from being Sara's Watcher. I did it once. You could, too."

She swallowed and looked down at her hands. "And who would protect her? Jak?"

"Jak is more than competent with a sword, and there are others who could step into your place as well."

She could not rightfully deny either point.

He added, "But you don't trust any of them to take care of her, do you?"

"None, but you." Shaun looked at him again and smiled. "But your duty is to Myra. I could never ask you to step aside from your duties to her for Sara."

Shaun turned her gaze back to the fire. If she was honest with herself, the idea of a relationship—with anyone, let alone Sara—had never even occurred to her. Anytime she reflected on her future, she thought about becoming a knight and serving her kingdom.

And protecting Sara. Always, she also thought about Sara.

Was Thomas right? Would she have to choose between being Sara's Watcher and admitting she had feelings for Sara?

Shaun shook her head. She did not know whether Sara felt the same for her, and she would not jeopardize her position or her friendship with Sara to find out.

"I am all Sara has right now. I won't abandon her."

Thomas nodded. She could not read his face, whether he disapproved or not. "You should rest. I'll take the first watch."

Shaun pushed herself to her feet. "Wake me when you want to turn in." She glanced over at the wagon, then said, "Please don't say anything to Sara."

He looked up at her. "I would never do that to you."

"I know. I just—I wanted to say it, in case you thought saying something to her would make things between her and I better somehow. I need to focus on keeping her safe. That's it."

"I know."

She studied his face. "Are we alright?"

Thomas sighed but nodded all the same. "But don't lie to me anymore."

She nodded back.

"Yes. We're fine then. Go sleep."

"Goodnight then."

Shaun walked back to the wagon, forcing herself not to limp, though the cold seemed to have seeped into her wounded leg and left a strange numbness there. The ground beneath the axles was still dry, but it had no warmth to offer her.

She pulled the blanket over her head and hugged it tight around her body. As she lay there, she begged for sleep to find her and take away her fear and doubt.

Sara needed her strength now.

17

COLD dawn light covered the hollow as Shaun roused the others. She kept the blanket Sara gave her the night before wrapped around her shoulders. The rain had continued through her night's watch and into the first stirrings of dawn. At times it made the pain in her leg worse, but just before dawn, the pain faded to a dull ache. A deep cold settled its place, filling her until not even the blanket could stop her shivering.

The others looked out at the dawn blearily. None of them said much as they shook off their sleep. Shaun could feel their tension, matched by her own.

Sara asked no one in particular, "Are you hungry?"

All of them shook their heads.

Shaun said, "We should make ready to leave for Parna. I'll gather the horse and get her settled in her bindings." She started to walk away.

Sara called out, "I can stow your blanket with the others, if you'd like."

Shaun did not turn back. "I'll hold onto it."

Thomas blurted out, "Shaun is sick."

She stopped, closing her eyes as she silently cursed him.

The steps at the back of the wagon creaked. Sara asked behind her, "Shaun? Is this true?"

She turned back as another tremor shook her. "Yes. Fine. I'm ill. The bite . . . it got infected. Or maybe it was poisoned. I don't know."

Sara came to stand in front of her, her eyes searching Shaun's face. "Were you sick yesterday? When I asked and you told me you were alright?"

Shaun looked away. "Yes. And I lied to you. I didn't want you to worry."

"Oh, Shaun. You knew I was worried already. Lying to me was better in your mind?"

Shaun said nothing.

Sara put a hand on Shaun's face and said softly, "You have a fever. You should lie down in the wagon and try to sleep. Myra or I can ride with Thomas."

Shaun pulled away. "*No*. I won't have either of you vulnerable like that. Not for me."

"Shaun—"

"*No.*" She turned away before Sara could say more.

Thomas murmured something, but Shaun kept walking.

The mare bent her head to nuzzle Shaun's shoulder as she untied the rope Thomas had used to hobble her. The mare snorted when Shaun did not respond. When she stood up again, she stroked the horse's brown and white speckled neck.

She murmured, "I pray the journey ahead is easy. For you as much as us."

If they were walking into a trap . . .

Shaun shook her head, refusing to finish the sentence, even in her own mind. She pulled up the stake on the other end of the rope and led the mare back to the front of the wagon.

Thomas was with Myra near the soggy remains of

the campfire. She seemed to be checking the bandages on his shoulder. Sara sat away from them, on the steps at the back of the wagon, brushing out her blond tresses. Her dark eyes stared off into the woods. Shaun paused to watch her.

Even in the rain, Sara still managed to look like royalty. Shaun, on the other hand, looked as disreputable as the lowest of thieves. Blood and dirt and river water stained her tunic and leggings. Her sword needed a good sharpening, one she could not get from the pitted, ancient whetstone she found in the wagon. Even the woolen blanket around her shoulders was speckled with bits of dead leaves.

She looked away from Sara and tugged on the mare's halter, leading her to her place in front of the wagon. Shaun's shaking fingers worked to refasten Thomas's makeshift bindings.

Sara came around the front of the wagon. She stood on the other side of the horse, running her fingers through the horse's mane, watching Shaun.

Shaun glanced at her and said quickly, "If you have come to ask me again to stand down—"

"I haven't."

Shaun nodded.

"I came to ask if you need help."

Shaun stopped and angrily balled up her shaking fingers. *"I don't."* She rested her hands on the mare's back. Hanging her head, she took a deep breath, then said, "I'm sorry. I'm just cold."

Sara's hands covered hers. Shaun looked into Sara's eyes as wet strands of her short hair blew across her face, caught by the wind.

Sara whispered, "It's alright."

"It's not. I am letting you and everyone else down."

She started to pull her hands away from Sara's, but Sara squeezed them more tightly, refusing to let her go. Her breath caught in her chest. She tried to slow the beating in her chest but could not.

Sara's eyes bore into hers. "You aren't letting me down."

Shaun nodded and let Sara hold her hands a moment longer, holding onto her warmth. Then she whispered, "I need to keep working."

Sara let go finally. Shaun turned her attention back to the bindings, again willing the pounding in her chest to stop. She shook the hair out of her eyes, trying to focus on the ropes, not Sara.

Whatever she might feel, she needed to push it down inside her as far as she could. The king charged her with keeping his daughter safe. She could not do that if she was distracted by some silly notion that was probably just in her head.

Sara asked, "What if we get to Parna and find that very few of our people made it out of Riverend?"

Shaun finished tying the bindings and patted the horse's shoulder. She repeated what she had been telling herself since they fled the city. "We have reserve forces throughout the other towns in the kingdom. We will make do with whatever soldiers we have at our disposal."

"Soldiers aren't a kingdom."

Shaun frowned. "What do you mean?"

"I am talking about my family, your parents, Thomas's and Myra's families, our artists, our diplomats, our scholars. Our *people*, Shaun. We need more than soldiers to save our kingdom."

Shaun looked into the woods. Sara was right. Soldiers made an army, not a kingdom.

"What if it's all gone?"

Shaun shook her head. "I don't know."

A frown crossed Sara's face. It was not the answer Sara wanted, but it was the only one Shaun had.

She was the daughter of fighters, not of a king and queen. Shaun knew how to defend and destroy, not rebuild. Rebuilding what Mordwell took from them would be up to people like Sara, not her.

Crossing to the other side of the wagon, Shaun drew Sara into an embrace. She could be something more than just an apprentice knight for Sara, just for that moment. She could be the shoulder Sara needed.

"We'll figure everything out when the time comes."

Sara put her head on Shaun's chest and nodded.

Thomas cleared his throat behind them.

Shaun turned her head. A smile crossed his face and then was gone again.

"We should be on our way."

Shaun nodded and let go of Sara.

When Sara and Myra were settled in the wagon again, Shaun climbed up to the driver's bench. She nodded to Thomas and wrapped the blanket tightly around herself again. He turned the mare out of the hollow, back in the direction of the road.

Again, the road was clear and empty.

But by midday, the light rain had turned into a downpour that drummed on the roof of the wagon and the overhang shielding the driver's bench. The overhang kept the worst of the rain off her and Thomas, but the rain soaked their boots and leggings from the knee down. Her wet clothing did nothing to improve the cold that persisted or her mood as the condition of the road worsened. Mud slopped up the side of the wagon each time they hit a deep puddle or rut in the road.

When they came within sight of Mondross's Crossing, Thomas pulled the wagon off the road again. Shaun slipped off the blanket covering her and turned to climb down from the bench. Thomas grabbed her arm.

She told him. "I will scout ahead. You stay with Sara and Myra."

He shook his head. "I don't think that's a good idea."

"You're better able to fight than me right now. If the wagon is attacked or I am captured at the crossing, it is better if you are here to protect Myra and Sara, not me."

Thomas considered this and then sighed. "You're right."

She climbed down from the bench and jogged into the woods, creeping through the brush and over deadfalls to get to a place where she could clearly see the crossing. When she did, she frowned. No one was there.

A hard stone of apprehension formed in Shaun's gut. When she returned to the wagon and told Thomas, his frown matched hers.

She asked, "Are we riding into a trap?"

He stared down the road. "I don't know. Maybe."

"Is there another choice? Another way for us to reach Parna that we've not considered?"

Thomas shook his head, then looked at her, a glimmer of hope in his eye. "Maybe the king's men already secured the crossing."

"Maybe."

Then why not leave Riverend soldiers in place to hold it? She did not give voice to this thought as Thomas guided the horse and wagon back onto the road.

They crossed the river over the wide wooden bridge and turned onto the road that would take them straight into Parna. The Kerning fell behind them as the road wended away from the river's banks, deep into rolling woodlands.

The rain tapered off, but the thick cloud cover remained, and a stiff breeze blew from the east. It carried the tang of salted seas with it. Shaun told herself that it was merely her imagination that more ominous clouds were gathering farther down the road in the direction of Parna. The stone of apprehension inside her spun itself into a boulder.

But the clouds did thicken the farther they got to Parna and the wind's intensity increased. The stone of apprehension inside her spun itself into a boulder. The speckled mare suddenly shook her head and snorted in agitation. Thomas cooed at her and the mare quieted some.

Then a crack of thunder shook the air. Shaun and Thomas jumped. The mare neighed and leapt into gallop. She pulled to the left, yanking the wagon with her. The leather strap holding Shaun and Thomas to the bench snapped taut as the mare's sudden shift threw them sideways. Shaun grabbed the rail above her to keep from tipping over the side of the bench. Sara and Myra screamed inside the covered wagon.

Thomas shouted at the horse, "Whoa! *Easy*."

Gritting his teeth, he fought to steer the horse away from the edge of the road. The wheels struck a rock and bounced the whole rig up. His knuckles went white as pulled back on the reins, repeating "whoa" until the horse finally slowed down.

Thomas got the mare to come to a full stop, but she pawed at the ground, looking like she might bolt again at any moment. He threw the hand brake into place in an attempt to keep the horse from taking the wagon with her if she did. His eyes were wide when he looked at Shaun.

Before he could say anything, she nodded, and turned to climb down again. The horse had taken them as far as she could. They were on their own now.

Thomas murmured softly as he approached the horse. She did not buck, but nor did she settle. She shifted in her bindings as he stroked her neck.

Shaun turned to the back of the wagon and tapped on the door. Sara opened it. She and Myra were both wide-eyed and huddled together on the wagon floor.

Sara asked, "What is going on?"

Shaun replied, "We walk from here."

18

THOMAS cut the mare loose from her bindings and slapped her on the hindquarters. She galloped away into the woods. Shaun watched her flee and wondered if the mare was giving them a warning they should heed. She paused, then pulled on her mail shirt and bracer and resettled her sword belt around her waist.

The gravel-covered road still bore the ruts and deep puddles from the rain. Shaun and the others walked through the grass instead. She could not help but feel that the woodlands were trying to press in on them as the thunder continued to rumble overhead. With each new rumble, Shaun's shoulders tightened more.

She slowed her pace as the road wound up a hill and looked up at the gray clouds overhead. Her brow furrowed. The clouds were not drifting across the sky. Rather, they looked to be moving in a slow rotational pattern.

A bolt of red lightning split the sky over the hill with a deafening crack. A deep growl of thunder followed, like some beast awakening. All four of them ducked with the sound.

Icy fear shot through Shaun's body as she watched the angry red fork dissipate and another shoot down toward the ground on the other side of the rise. It was happening again. The realization ignited something in Shaun.

"No. *No!*" The lightning ignited something in Shaun. She broke into a jog and then a run, pushing through the ache and weakness in her legs. The others shouted her name, but she refused to stop.

She ran toward the top of the rise, heart pounding in her ears. The pounding muffled the shouting behind her and the rasping of her own breath. When she crested the rise, she came to a slow stop. Her mouth dropped open in horror.

A bloody scene stretched below her, across the fields outside Parna's gates. The battered standards of Riverend flew over a shifting mass of green, black, and red as Riverend soldiers fought ranks of Mordwellians. She could hear the clash of swords against shields and the screams of the dying. She imagined she could smell the blood, too.

Shaun broke into a run again, down the hill. Her boots slid on the wet grass and mud, and she stumbled, but kept going. Getting downhill was easier than going up. She picked up speed as she descended. But not enough.

Thomas shouted her name. His boots pounded on the hill behind her, the sound growing louder as he closed the distance. She tried to run faster, but Thomas tackled her from behind and pulled her to the ground. The wind rushed out of her when she fell.

They tumbled down the hillside in a tangle of limbs. When they finally rolled to a stop, Shaun gasped for breath and shoved Thomas.

"Get off me!"

He let go of her and got up. She glared at him as she stood as well.

He shouted, "Stop this! What is the matter with you?"

She gestured at the scene behind her. "Do you not see them? They're all *dying*!" She doubled over, choking back tears. Her worst nightmare had just come to pass.

Sara and Myra caught up to them. Tears rolled down Myra's face. Sara shouted, "Stop fighting each other!"

She looked at the scene behind Shaun. Her eyes searched it again and again. Sara's face turned as desperate as Shaun felt. Her lips quivered. *"My father."* Sara's gaze turned to Shaun and Thomas. "We have to do something. We have to find my father."

Thomas shook his head. "We need to get you and Myra out of here and find safety elsewhere."

"No." Tears streamed down Sara's face. Her eyes locked onto Shaun's. "Shaun, please. *Do something.* We must find my father. We cannot leave without him. Riverend needs him."

Thomas was still shaking his head. But where did he expect them to go? Where in Riverend would be safe enough for them?

Shaun's fevered mind struggled between the king's order to protect Sara echoing through her mind and Sara's words. The words of the king's daughter.

Thomas saw the conflict in her and grabbed her arm. "Remember the king's orders. Remember your duty."

Her duty was to follow the king's orders and keep Sara safe. It was also to obey the wishes of her Ward. The fact that her Ward was the king's daughter gave those wishes double weight. The time had come for her to choose whether to obey the king or obey Sara. Her eyes met Thomas's.

"*I am* thinking of my duty. And Sara's right."

"Shaun—"

"We need King Jaris. Without him, Riverend will be too weak to stand. Nowhere in the Ten Kingdoms will be safe enough for Sara or Myra. You know this, Thomas. Take them away from here. I'll search for the king and then find you."

Thomas frowned, but did not try to block her as she pushed past him. She yanked her sword free of its scabbard as she ran toward the battle.

A low ceiling of black clouds swirled over the center of the battle, nearly obscuring the daylight. Another arc of red lightning cut across the dark sky. The mass of green and black resolved into Riverend and Mordwellian soldiers locked in a death match.

Enemies filled Shaun's vision. Everywhere, pale soldiers in black armor tore at the dying with swords and their bare teeth. Shaun's insides twisted, sickened by the abominations before her. She dove into the tangle, swinging her sword at the nearest Mordwellian within her reach.

When she cut down the first, she pressed ahead, seeking out the next. She fought the weakness in her limbs, gripping her sword tighter as a thick metallic soup of blood and fear filled her nose. Rage grew in her, fed by the screams of the wounded. She fell blind to everything but her need to kill every last Mordwellian on her way to the king.

A knight tumbled from his white charger ahead of her, a spear thrust through a gap in his armor. A black armored soldier rushed toward him. She shouted, running to intercept the Mordwellian.

He stopped and turned toward her. She expected to

look into the dead eyes of one of Mordwell's creatures, but she found herself looking into the eyes of an ordinary man. He laughed at her surprise and dove at her. Shaun cut his head from his shoulders.

The knight was already dead when she bent next to him. His charger danced back a step when Shaun approached her. But she did not shy from Shaun when she caught the horse's reins.

Shaun pulled herself up into the saddle and turned the horse deeper into the fray, searching for the king. She spotted a group of Riverend standards farther in and kicked the charger into a gallop toward them. The charger became her battering ram as they plunged through the crowd. But the press of soldiers was soon too thick for the charger to maneuver through. Shaun pulled her sword free again, swinging down at the Mordwellians surrounding them.

There seemed to be no end to them. Her sword arm started to go numb from exertion. Panic rose in her throat when a Mordwellian caught hold of her boot and tried to yank her out of the saddle. She slipped to the side with his tug, but grabbed hold of the saddle's horn with her free hand. The charger reared up and spun around, knocking the Mordwellian and two others away. Shaun pressed herself against the horse, desperate to keep her seat.

When the charger's front hooves thundered back down, Shaun sheathed her sword with shaking hands and turned the horse away from the center of the battle. She could find no clear path to the Riverend standards she could still see flying.

With a growl, Shaun kicked the charger into a gallop in the direction where she thought she had entered the battle. She slowed the horse to a trot at the battle's edge, turning her one way and then the other, still searching for an opening. Finally, she stopped.

She could not reach the king.

The only thing waiting for her at the center of the battle was death. Purposely riding into an unwinnable battle would serve neither her king nor Sara well. It was time for her to abandon her search and trust those around the king to get him to safety. She needed to find Sara and the others.

Standing in the stirrups, she looked for a sign of which way Thomas had taken Sara and Myra. She could see nothing at first but the dead strewn across the field. Fear gripped her heart as she wondered if they were captured.

Then she saw movement at the edge of the woodlands opposite the hillside they descended from. Shaun dropped back into the saddle and kicked the horse into a sprint in the direction of the three figures running for the cover of the woods.

Thomas and the others disappeared into the trees. Shaun frowned and aimed the charger for where they disappeared into the woods. At the edge of the trees, she slowed the horse to a trot.

The light in the woods was faint as falling twilight. Shaun squinted and ducked as her mount passed under a low branch. She saw no one ahead of her or to the left or right. They could not have vanished into thin air . . .

She took a deep breath, then quietly hissed, "Sara? Thomas?"

Nothing. Then, "Shaun?"

She turned her head to see Sara and Myra poke their

heads out from behind a broad, rotted-out tree trunk. Thomas emerged from under a fallen log he had been tucked under. She breathed a sigh of relief.

Sara came to stand next to the charger. She took Shaun's hand. "Are you alright?"

Shaun hung her head. "Yes, but I couldn't reach your father. I'm sorry. I tried. There were just too many Mordwellians between us."

"Did you at least see him? Did he look alright?"

"I—" A chill ran up Shaun's spine and the hairs on the back of her neck stood on end. Her brow furrowed.

"Shaun?"

Her eyes searched the woods. She saw movement deep within the trees. *Mordwellian soldiers!*

"Thomas!"

Her hands fell to her sword. Then she heard a high-pitched whistle. Something struck a nearby tree trunk. Bark flew off of the trunk in a sharp spray, making Shaun and Sara duck.

Another whistle.

"Thomas! Get—"

A projectile slammed into her left shoulder, piercing her chainmail. It spun her out of the saddle. She cried out in pain when she landed on her shoulder, onto whatever struck her.

Sara cried her name, but the charger suddenly reared up, knocking Sara backward. The horse shot forward and narrowly missed Shaun with her back hooves. A bolt struck the horse in the chest as she galloped toward the Mordwellians. She screamed in pain as blood spurted over her white coat.

Shaun let herself roll onto her back, staring at the

branches above her as she gasped for air through the pain in her shoulder and her upper back. Sweat bathed her face. Her shaking fingers reached up to feel for what hit her. They wrapped around a metal crossbow bolt. The barbs on its head were buried deep in her flesh. She could feel them every time she gasped in a breath.

Far away, Myra screamed Thomas's name. Shaun told herself she had to get up, but she could barely breathe, let alone move.

Sara's face came into view. Her eyes were red with tears and panic. They lighted on the bolt in Shaun's shoulder and the blood soaking her tunic.

"Oh, gods, Shaun." Her hands shook when she reached for the bolt.

Shaun gasped out, "*No*. Leave it. You have to run."

Without intervention, the wound in her shoulder would probably kill her. She was in no shape to help Sara now. Sara had to escape without her while Sara still could.

But her eyes hardened. "No. I won't run. I won't leave you here to die."

Myra screamed again. Sara's head turned in the direction from which Myra's scream came. When she looked back at Shaun, she squeezed her hand.

"I need to help Myra. Try not to move. I'll return for you." She jumped to her feet.

Without thinking, Shaun twisted, trying to grab Sara's hand. She missed and fell, gasping for breath as she watched Sara run toward the fray between Myra, Thomas, and the Mordwellians.

Shaun rolled onto her back again. Gritting her teeth, she wrapped her fingers tight around the bolt. She took as deep a breath as she could manage and closed her eyes, whispering to herself that she could pull it out. *She had to.*

She tugged. The bolt barely moved before white hot pain shot down her shoulder and arm. She screamed and let her hand drop, balling it into a fist. She sobbed and pounded the ground until the pain lessened again.

When she opened her eyes again, she looked for Sara and the others. Thomas was missing. The charger was lying on the ground, motionless. The Mordwellians had surrounded Myra and Sara. They dragged Myra away from Sara, deeper into the woods.

Sara kicked and swung at the two soldiers trying to grab her. Then she broke into a run in Shaun's direction. The Mordwellians caught her and lifted her off her feet.

No matter how much it would hurt, Shaun knew she had to get up. She could not let them take Sara.

Shaun forced herself onto her side and up on one arm, screaming through the pain. Dark spots formed at the edges of her vision. She got to her knees. A wave of dizziness rocked her. She squeezed her eyes shut, willing herself to keep going, and tried to stand, but stumbled back to her knees. Through her darkening vision, she saw Sara twist in the soldiers' grip. She screamed something as they pulled her away, but Shaun could not understand her.

Then her view was cut off by a wall of black. Shaun realized it was four Mordwellians running toward her. They surrounded her and two of them yanked Shaun to her feet. Her breathing came short and fast. The Mordwellians smiled hungrily at her. One of them grabbed hold of the bolt in her shoulder.

"No, don't!"

He grinned and yanked the metal bolt out. Her knees buckled with the agony, and darkness finally found her.

19

THE SHOULDER in her stomach woke her, and the world tilted crazily as Shaun was hauled off her feet and turned upside-down. Her eyes opened and focused on the black leather-covered back in front of her face. She turned her head slightly to see three other Mordwellians, one of whom carried her mail shirt, sword, and belt. Her hands were now bound behind her.

Pain shot down her wounded shoulder with each movement the fourth soldier made as he carried her, but without the bolt lodged in it, drawing breath was less painful. With each breath, the metallic smell of her own blood filled her nose. Blood dripped off her shoulder, onto her face and her hair. Shaun closed her eyes to feign unconsciousness and keep blood out of them.

One of the soldiers said something in guttural Mordwellian. The one holding her stopped and bent forward, dumping her on the ground again. She could not fight back a cry when she landed.

"Shaun!"

She turned her head to see Sara next to her, also bound and kneeling. Myra knelt on the other side of her, and Thomas lay next to Myra. Neither Sara nor Myra appeared to have more than bruises, but Thomas's eyes were closed and dark rivulets of blood ran down his tan skin from a head wound.

Shaun struggled upright, ignoring the spots that appeared at edge of her vision again. Relief washed over her when she saw Thomas's chest rise and fall. At least he was still alive.

This was her fault. Going after the king had been a fool's errand. She left them all open to capture. She should have listened to Thomas.

Shaun shoved her guilt aside for the moment and turned her attention to their surroundings and their captors. The Mordwellians had gathered them in a narrow clearing deep in the woods. They stood in a ring around Shaun and the others, staring at them. The trees' shadows had grown long and fell over the Mordwellians' faces.

A new figure, not a Mordwellian, stepped into view. He smirked at them. "What an interesting little party we have gathered here."

Shaun's mouth fell open as recognition hit her between the eyes. All the pieces began to fall into place.

Sara shouted, "Traitor."

Castian Krieger, Darcy's father, laughed. "A title I wear proudly these days."

The high duke's smug look matched the one Shaun had seen on his daughter just days ago. He strolled into the center of the group, readjusting the sable half-cape draped around his shoulders. His oiled black hair still had its usual, crisp part down its middle and his beard looked like it had been recently trimmed.

No blood or dirt from the battle outside Parna sullied his clothes or hands. Shaun had no doubt that he had watched the slaughter all the same.

Another figure hovered deep in the growing shadows behind Krieger. Shaun could not make out more than a hint of dark robes to identify him.

Sara demanded, "How could you sell your own people out to the Mordwellians?"

"With pleasure." His eyes went to Shaun. "I must thank you for giving us the king's daughter. If we had not seen you running across the field, as foolhardy as any true Riverend knight, we might never have noticed her. The high minister's daughter was an added bonus."

His head tilted. "Isn't it your duty to die defending her?"

Shaun dropped her gaze. He was not wrong. She had acted rashly. By giving away their position so easily, she had dishonored her position as Watcher.

"My daughter was right—your emotions get the better of you far too much." A sneer passed over Krieger's face. He reached forward and tugged at the Riverend insignia on the low collar of her tunic. "Only the pride and arrogance of a Riverend knight would make you believe you could take on so many of Mordwell's best fighters on your own. And all for nothing. Riverend belongs to Mordwell now."

Shaun spat in his face. Krieger scowled and stepped back. He wiped the spittle from his cheek with a square of black silk and tossed it aside. Then he backhanded her across the face. She fell onto her injured shoulder and barely stifled a cry as pain shot down her shoulder and arm.

Sara shouted, "Leave her alone!"

"She will learn, *all* of you will learn, not disrespect your betters. You stay alive only at our pleasure now, *Princess.* We intend to use you to our full advantage in securing the unconditional surrender of Riverend's royal line."

"My father will never surrender. He will come for us."

Krieger laughed. "You are half right. We've already met with the king. We captured him right here in Parna."

Sara shook her head. "No. That's not possible."

"I had hoped he would see the sense in negotiating a full surrender in the face of the overwhelming odds against his armies. But he refused, even when my Mordwellian friends began flaying the skin from his arms."

Sara gagged and Shaun's stomach turned over in kind.

"A fully *infuriating* and disagreeable man, your father. Sadly, my friends do not like the word 'no'. They tried to change his mind until they had bled him dry. I would have intervened, since he was worth more to us alive than dead, but I have learned it is best not to interrupt when they are having their fun. However, I did manage to save his head. I plan to have it stuffed."

Sara slumped forward. Her shoulders shook with her sobbing. Shaun forced herself upright again.

"Shut your mouth, Krieger."

His gaze went from Sara to Shaun. "I will do no such thing. You and she should both know how little Jaris Hahlerand—any of the Hahlerands, nay, anyone in the Ten Kingdoms—deserve your tears. They brought this on themselves, always too arrogant for their own good. Did you really think the little treaty they negotiated would solve everything? It just delayed the inevitable. I knew this, but Jaris never listened.

"Perhaps if his father had not outlawed sorcery in Riverend, the kingdom would not have been left so unprepared for what was to come. The sorcerers of Mordwell simply bided their time, gathering strength until they could usurp the Mackritaes' power. They wield superior powers to anything Riverend has to offer. For just a taste of that power and the respect Jaris never gave me, I handed Riverend to them."

Shaun struggled against the bindings on her wrists, wanting nothing less than to smash Krieger in his smug face. But the ropes held fast and her struggles only made her wounds bleed more. Fresh blood soaked her shirt sleeve.

The figure behind Krieger said something in Mordwellian. Krieger looked back at him. The man stepped out of the shadows and approached them. His pallor shocked her.

His skin was nearly translucent and his limbs were stick-thin. No hair covered his head. A pair of unnaturally blue eyes burned into her from his hooded eye sockets. Symbols she did not recognize underlined each of his eyes. Others decorated his smooth scalp and flowed down the sides of his neck. Animal bones affixed to the collar and sleeves of his jet-black robes clicked together when he walked. A palpable aura of power surrounded him.

Shaun wondered if he was some kind of undead creature—a lich maybe.

He came to stand in front of her. Bony hands emerged from the sleeves of his robes and his claw-like fingers brushed against her bleeding shoulder. He muttered a few words. A burning sensation formed at the center of her wound and spread across her shoulder.

Shaun bit back a cry. She could smell her own flesh burning. There came a sudden pop and a flash of smoke, followed by a sharp stinging in her shoulder. She let out a curse and bowed forward.

Sara cried out, "Stop! You're hurting her."

Slowly, the pain faded and the bleeding from her shoulder stopped. The Mordwellian spoke again in his guttural tongue. He gestured to the guards around them.

Rough hands grabbed her and pulled her to her feet. The sorcerer stepped even closer to her. She gagged at the pungent smell of decay on him, though she could not tell if it came from him or something on his person.

His unnatural eyes burned into hers, hypnotic. He sniffed at her once and then again. His gaze went down to her boots. A joyless grin spread across his face. He looked at the soldiers holding her, nodding. They tightened their grip.

Sweat beaded on her forehead as the sorcerer grinned at her. He squatted down and grabbed hold of the boot on her injured leg. She tried to pull away, but the guards held her too tightly. He sliced through her laces with a bone-handled dagger and yanked off her boot.

His sharp nails dug into her ankle as he pulled her leg toward him. Red and black lines now emanated from the bite wound on her leg, stretching partway up her calf. He chuckled softly as he caressed them. Then he looked back at Krieger and said something in Mordwellian.

Krieger made a tisking sound. "My pale friend says you've been bitten by one of his creatures. Do you know what this means?"

Shaun said nothing, swallowing hard.

"You will never become a knight of Riverend, but you will be lucky enough to serve Mordwell."

"What are you talking about?"

"You are going to become like the creature that bit you. The venom in their bite just starts the process. There's much more in store for you still."

Icy fear shot through her. *"No."*

Krieger gave her a mirthless smile. "They call it the 'eternal nightmare'. A special hell reserved for their enemies and prisoners of war. You will be at the mercy of your master, bound by him to commit whatever terrible acts he chooses. As I understand it, you will still be aware of what you're doing, but unable to stop yourself, like a nightmare that only death can wake you from. I think it's a fitting end for you."

The sorcerer stood again. Shaun tightened her jaw, even as her heart began to pound. She refused to beg for her life.

He produced a crimson leather pouch and dug his fingers into the contents. He threw them at her. A cloud of glittering dust struck her chest and wafted up into her face, choking her as it filled her nose and mouth.

Dizziness washed over her. Her face went numb first, then the rest of her body. She heard Sara calling for her from somewhere far away. Shaun managed to gasp out Sara's name before she lost consciousness.

20

SHAUN slowly became aware she was lying on a cold slab in a dark place. She could not make out any details to tell her where she was, nor could she tell whether she was asleep or awake. Claw-like hands traced over her body and pulled at her limbs. Shadows bent toward her. Burning red orbs that could have been eyes stared down at her from the shadows' depths.

Lightning flashed overhead. It seemed to ignite a ring of candles around her. They flickered wildly as a cold wind scented with incense and wood smoke blew across her exposed form.

Chanting filled her ears, coming from an unseen source. It rose and fell in guttural tones. Her skin suddenly burned as something snaked across it. She tried to cry out for Sara—where was she—but found she could not. Her voice and her body no longer obeyed her.

Something warm dripped on her face. Blood.

The darkness faded. She then found herself standing once again on the killing fields outside of Parna. Everyone was dead but her. The strange clouds still churned overhead and red lighting scarred the sky.

The clouds took the shape of the dark sorcerer's face. Lightning shot from his eyes. His cloud mouth opened up, and a whirlwind was born within it. It tugged at her, pulling her toward it.

Shaun struggled to keep her footing. She threw herself to the ground and dug her fingernails into the blood-soaked ground. Even pinned flat to the fetid mud, the whirlwind pulled at her, and she knew she could not fight it for long. The sorcerer's laughter echoed around her.

The wind intensified and its roar grew until it deafened her, drowning out even the laughter. Her grip began to weaken. Her legs lifted off the ground, then her hands came loose. She flew up into the sorcerer's mouth.

Sara screamed her name.

Shaun sat up, gasping for air.

Someone grabbed her arm. She struck out blindly. Whoever grabbed her ducked just out of her reach.

Sara hissed at her, "Shaun, wake up!"

She blinked until her vision cleared and she could see Sara sitting at her feet. She lay on a bed of straw in a tent.

"Calm down. You're safe now." Sara paused and corrected herself. *"Safer."*

Shaun said nothing. There was nothing for her to be calm about. She felt a wrongness in her, deep inside, a cold that was less a sensation than a thought. Her arms still burned. What she had hoped was just a nightmare was not. Something had been done to her.

She looked down at herself. Both her arms were bandaged. She did not remember why. Her own tunic was gone, replaced with a dark one. Her injured shoulder and forearm, at least, no longer bothered her. Neither did her leg.

Only her burning arms bothered her now. And the cold.

Shaun glanced past Sara at the rest of the tent. It was only large enough to accommodate three straw beds with not much more than a pace between them. Daylight lit the dark tent walls. Myra sat next to Thomas, who was chained to the tent's center support. Both of them stared at her.

Thomas's head was bandaged and he had a deep bruise under his right eye. Two of his fingers were taped together, broken perhaps.

Sara said her name. Her eyes went back to Sara.

"Are you alright?"

"How long was I unconscious?"

"Two days, I think. You were unconscious when they brought you back to us last night." Sara whispered, "They took you away after you blacked out. Where did they take you?"

Shaun shook her head. "I can't remember."

"I wasn't sure I would see you again."

She nodded, unsure what else to do or say to this. Any feelings she might have had about Sara's obvious concern for her were now gone. She asked, "Where are we? Why are my arms bandaged?"

"We're in the Mordwellians' camp outside Parna." Sara paused again. "There's something you should see."

She rose and resettled next to her. Shaun noticed a large bruise on Sara's cheek. It looked fresh.

She caught Sara's wrist as she reached for Shaun. "Who gave that bruise to you?"

Sara hesitated before she said, "Krieger."

Shaun's jaw tightened. A rage deeper than any she had felt before slowly built inside her as she thought of Krieger striking Sara. She would kill him for it.

Sara laid her hand over Shaun's. "Don't worry about that now."

She slowly unraveled the bandages covering Shaun's left arm and then her right. Black marks—symbols like those on the sorcerer's face and neck—covered both her wrists and forearms. Sara pushed Shaun's sleeve up. Her touch did nothing to cool the fire on Shaun's skin. If anything, it burned hotter, but she did not stop Sara.

The symbols continued up to her shoulder. The spidery lines twisted one with another. Red at the edges of the tattooed lines made them look poisonous.

Sara asked, "What do they mean?"

Shaun shook her head as she stared at them. She half expected them to start moving like snakes before her eyes.

"I'm scared, Shaun. Krieger has brought me to his tent twice now, mostly to threaten me and claim they are close to capturing the rest of my family. I don't believe any of it. But he's also told me that the sorcerer who took you away is the leader of some dark order of Mordwellian sorcerers. They overthrew and executed most of the Mackritae ruling family.

"He spends much of his time in Krieger's tent, probably wary that Krieger will have a change of heart about what they're doing. He wants to reintegrate Decathea under his order's rule. Smaller kingdoms west of the Golden Peaks have already fallen under Mordwellian control, before Riverend did."

"How have we not heard of this?"

Sara shook her head. "I know not. Krieger keeps bragging about how strong the sorcerers of Mordwell are, saying they're virtually unstoppable because of their . . . thralls, those creatures we encountered outside Riverend's walls. The ones that bit you." She shuddered. "I am frightened for you."

Thomas added, "We need to get out of here. We can plan our escape, now that you're awake."

Sara nodded. "From things Krieger has said, I've gathered that Fredrik escaped the slaughter at Parna, along with other members of my family. I don't know how, but we must get out of here and find him."

Jaris's third oldest son. Shaun remembered him having a good head on his shoulders. She did not trust herself to still protect Sara. Fredrik, however, could get Sara to safety.

Sara went on. "I don't know how much of my family might still be alive, nor how much of our forces remain. Krieger has said very few, but I know he is just trying to break me. If we can get to Fredrik, I know he must have a plan for taking back the capitol and the rest of our kingdom."

Shaun nodded. "But you must leave me here."

Sara's brow wrinkled. "What? No. We're not leaving without you."

The cold and the anger Shaun felt building inside her were foreign enemies. They meant nothing good for Sara, Thomas, or Myra. She did not know how long she could control what was happening to her. She would only endanger Sara and the others, if she went with them.

Shaun looked at Thomas. "If I am with you, you will be in danger. I cannot allow anymore harm to come to any of you because of me. You need to leave me here."

"No." Sara clasped Shaun's hands. "I have already lost my father and gods know how much of the rest of my family. I cannot lose you, too. I need you."

Shaun looked down at their entwined hands, barely feeling the affection for Sara that had been inside her before. She pulled Sara into an embrace. It would be their last. She wanted to give Sara something good to remember, even if all she felt was pain when Sara's body touched hers.

21

SARA screamed for help. She and Myra knelt on either side of Thomas. The tent flap flew open and two Mordwellian soldiers entered. They paused just inside to stare at Thomas's limp form at the center of the tent. His head lolled to one side and blood trickled from his mouth.

Myra cried, "Don't just stand there! He needs help."

The guards stepped farther into the tent. The lead guard asked in slow Common, "What is wrong with him?"

Sara said, "I don't know. He started coughing and then slumped over. You need to get him help."

The other guard looked over at Shaun's empty straw bed. His hand fell to the sword at his hip. "Where the other one?"

"Behind you."

Shaun stepped out from the shadows by the tent entrance as the guards spun around. She leapt forward and grabbed the guard in front of her, snapping his neck with a violent twist of his head. Behind him, Sara stifled a scream with her hands over her mouth.

As the dead man fell, Shaun grabbed hold of his sword's hilt. The other guard opened his mouth to shout, but she ran him through before he could get it out. Their eyes met.

A sickening combination of inhuman rage and glee filled her as she stared into the Mordwellian's shocked face. He gasped for air around the sword in his chest.

When his knees gave out, she grabbed the front of his tunic and let him fall softly. His mouth worked, but still no sound but gasping came out of him. She leaned over him, watching him until he took his last breath and his eyes glazed over. Only then did she pull the sword free.

She stood, bloody sword in hand. "It won't be long before someone notices these two are gone."

Myra snagged the keys for Thomas's shackles off the belt of the guard whose neck was broken. She unlocked the shackles on Thomas's wrists with shaking hands. He rubbed at them while Myra unlocked the shackles on his ankles.

Sara, however, stayed motionless next to Thomas, staring at Shaun with a mixture of horror and fear. She seemed to realize this after a moment and dropped her gaze. Shaun turned away.

Her hands shook for a moment. She tightened her grip on the sword and balled her other hand into a fist. Something inside her liked watching that man die. Her own horror at this knowledge matched what she saw on Sara's face.

What was happening to her?

Shaun turned back to the others when the last of Thomas's shackles fell with a clink. Myra helped him stand and he shook out his arms and legs. He rubbed his jaw where Shaun had hit him to make the ruse more convincing. "That really hurt, by the way."

"Sorry."

He nodded, but looked like he wondered if she truly was. Even she wondered that.

Thomas moved toward the tent's entrance. "Let's go, while we still can."

Shaun stopped him. "I say again: you should leave me behind."

Sara shook her head, though Shaun noticed it was with less adamance than before. "No. I won't leave you behind."

Shaun frowned and turned away, peeling back the tent flap. No other guards stood outside, and none of the Mordwellians she could see appeared to be watching the tent. They all seemed focused on other tasks. Groups of soldiers carried crates and sacks to wagons, while others broke down some of the tents.

When she closed the flap, she asked Sara, "Why are the Mordwellians breaking down camp?" She told the others what she saw.

Sara's brow furrowed, and she shook her head. "Krieger didn't mention anything that suggested we would be moving elsewhere."

Thomas rubbed his bruised face again. "We don't have a choice other than try to escape now. Shaun's right; someone is going to notice the guards are gone. We can use the camp break down as cover."

Shaun nodded. "We'll go two at a time, so we're less noticeable as we cross the camp."

Sara said, "I saw a horse corral the last time Krieger had me brought to his tent. It's not far from the edge of camp, but it is dangerously close to his tent. There are other tents nearby that we can use for cover."

Thomas asked, "How well guarded is the corral?"

"It looked unguarded."

Shaun and Thomas glanced at each other, thinking the same thing. Were the Mordwellians overconfident or were the horses purposely left unguarded?

Thomas pressed his lips into a thin line, then took a long, curved dagger from the guard Shaun stabbed. He slipped it into his belt. "Let us see how the situation looks when we get closer to the corral."

Shaun nodded. "You and Myra go first. I will follow with Sara."

She would get Sara to safety, then find a way to separate herself from the group. Staying behind was not an appealing option, but she would sacrifice herself to keep Sara safe from whatever was happening to her. What little affection for Sara remained inside her told her that was the right thing to do.

Sara told Thomas to head northeast from the tent. He nodded and took Myra's hand. Shaun counted to five after they slipped out, then she led Sara out. She let Thomas and Myra get several paces ahead, not moving from one cover spot to another until Thomas moved and safely reached the next tent.

Shaun spotted the corral. She looked around the stack of crates she and Sara were crouched behind and met Thomas's gaze. He gestured toward the corral and held up four fingers. She nodded.

On the count of four, he slipped out from behind the tent shielding him and Myra from the soldiers moving through the camp. Myra followed close behind him. They walked fast toward the horse corral.

A shout of alarm rose suddenly from somewhere behind Shaun and Sara's position. Thomas cursed. He broke into a run, pulling Myra with him.

Shaun gritted her teeth, then grabbed Sara's hand. "Come on!" She jumped out from behind the crates.

They sprinted across the open space between the crates and the horse corral. The flap on the large tent on the other side of the corral flew open. Krieger ran out. His mouth fell open in a mixture of surprise and fury.

In different circumstances, Shaun might have smiled. But then another figure stepped around Krieger.

The Mordwellian sorcerer.

Shaun let go of Sara's hand. "Keeping going!"

The sorcerer shouted a single word in Mordwellian. An inferno of pain seized Shaun's body. She cried out and fell, skidding to a stop on her knees.

Sara slowed to a stop and shouted for Thomas.

The tattoos on Shaun's arms flashed bright red. She tried to get up, but her body refused to obey. Some force held her fast. It pressed on her chest, making it hard for her to breathe. Shaun bowed her head, gasping.

Sara pleaded, "Shaun, you have to get up and run!"

But she could not answer. Out of the corner of her darkening vision, she saw Mordwellians running toward them.

Thomas shouted, "Sara! Run!"

"Not without Shaun!" Sara ran back to her.

Shaun gasped through gritted teeth, *"Run. Away."*

"I won't leave you. Just take my hand."

She managed to raise her head and look at Sara, growling, *"I don't want to hurt you."*

Sara reached for her. "Take my hand."

Thomas and Myra had stopped halfway between Sara and the horse corral. Thomas's eyes went to the

Mordwellians converging on Shaun and Sara and others advancing on him and Myra. Shaun saw him curse again before he turned and grabbed Myra, pulling her toward the corral. She wanted to tell him she was sorry, but the force holding her would not allow it.

More shouting came from the edge of the camp beyond the corral. Arrows soared through the air and rained down on the Mordwellians. The soldiers running toward Thomas and Myra stopped and fell back. Flaming arrows struck the tents.

Shouts from Krieger and the Mordwellians blended with the shouting at the edge of camp. She tried again to tell Sara to run, but cacophony of voices drowned out her words. Sara looked back toward the edge of the camp.

Soldiers wearing Riverend's colors poured into the encampment. But Shaun knew that help had come too late for them. Unbidden, Shaun's hand shot out and grabbed Sara's wrist. She pulled Sara down toward her.

Sara cried out in surprise and pain. "Shaun, *stop*. You're hurting me."

"I told you to run." Her own voice sounded flat, cold, and foreign to her.

Mordwellian soldiers surrounded Shaun and Sara, cutting them off from the Riverend soldiers. They did not attack Shaun or Sara. They shielded them.

Seemingly from nowhere, the dark sorcerer appeared behind Sara. Shaun closed her eyes as her other hand rose. It closed into a fist and struck Sara. Her eyes opened again as Sara fell. Tears spilled down Shaun's cheeks.

The Mordwellian sorcerer smiled. He stepped around Sara's unconscious form and spoke another word in his native tongue, tapping his fingers against Shaun's forehead. Shaun fell, pulled down into the darkness, and ceased to be.

22

SARA gasped and started to sit up, but the pounding in her head stopped her. She looked around. She was lying on a cot in a smaller tent than before. Night had fallen. A single lantern hanging at the tent's center barely lit the tent, its wick turned low. She could not see much past its feeble glowing.

Her face felt swollen. She slowly raised her hand to touch it where Shaun had struck her. Just her fingertips on the lump where the blow landed caused her pain. She let her hand drop. Her lips quivered as she struggled to understand what was happening.

She thought of the way Shaun spoke to her right before striking her. Her voice was so cold and flat. It was not Shaun's at all. What had the Mordwellians done to her?

Shaun was the strongest person she knew, other than her father. She pushed herself much harder than anyone around her, winning top marks during the Trials for her physical and mental fitness. What could the Mordwellians have done to corrupt her so? What had they done to make Shaun betray her?

Fear stabbed Sara's heart as she wondered if Shaun was lost to her forever. Her mind cycled back through all of the arguments they had over the past year, many of them because Sara could not understand what she had started to feel inside.

Their relationship had grown so complicated in Sara's mind. But Shaun had never seemed to notice, so wrapped up as she was in her training. Sara had punished Shaun for her blindness.

She had said Shaun never saw her. But then, what had she done to help Shaun see?

She had taken Shaun for granted. Only after the fall of Riverend had she realized how self-centered and shortsighted she had been during all those arguments. But then there never seemed to be a right moment for her to tell Shaun this.

Sara pushed herself up into a sitting position. Her throat felt dry and scratchy. She turned, looking for water. The tent flap suddenly opened and fell shut again as someone she had not seen before bolted out of the tent. She jumped.

Was it Shaun?

Sara called her name. No one answered.

Then Sara heard voices outside. The flap opened again and Krieger strolled in, followed by a pair of Mordwellian soldiers. They took up positions by the tent's entrance.

Krieger paced in the middle of the tent. Tufts of his hair stood out from the rest, as though he had run his fingers through it repeatedly. Sara got off her cot and stood. She would not lay down in the presence of a traitor to Riverend. That was not the Hahlerand way.

He muttered, "Your family is most troublesome."

Sara could not help but smile. He sneered at her.

"Laugh if you wish. I hope Fredrik enjoyed our little

trap." He stopped and smirked at her. "I hope you don't think you were overly clever, escaping from your guards and trying to reach the unguarded horses. Did you think we were so stupid as to leave them wide open to theft?

"The two guards that were killed, I assume by Shaun's hands, were a small price to pay to rid ourselves of one apprentice knight and a hostage we cannot use."

Sara swallowed. "What are you saying?"

"We only wanted you. Demoralizing Fredrik and his ragtag band of fighters made up from the last dregs of Riverend knights and a bunch of farmers playing soldier was a nice bonus. Pity we couldn't capture him while we were at it. We would surely have secured the surrender of Riverend with both you and he in our custody."

Sara lifted her chin in defiance. "Fredrik and the others will come back for us."

"Us? You don't mean Shaun, do you?" Krieger let out a mirthless laugh. "She is not going anywhere. In fact, she seems quite at home with us."

Krieger went to the tent's entrance and gestured to someone outside. Shaun walked into the tent, wearing leather armor bearing the seal of Mordwell. The dark sorcerer entered the tent with Shaun and stood behind her.

"Shaun?" Sara tried to keep the quaver from her voice but failed.

Shaun did not look at her. She did not even blink at the sound of Sara's voice. The sorcerer smiled grotesquely behind Shaun. His skeletal fingers played with the animal bones sewn to his black robes.

Krieger came to stand next to Sara. He leaned down and whispered, "Shaun is no more. What you see before you is a loyal soldier of Mordwell."

No. She closed her eyes a moment, willing herself not to cry. She tried again. "Wake up, Shaun. Please."

The sorcerer's grin broadened. The wickedness in his eyes made her recoil inside. He said something in Mordwellian. Shaun stepped forward and stood in front of her. Sara barely noticed when Krieger stepped back from her.

No spark of recognition lit Shaun's green eyes. They remained blank. Dead.

Her throat tightened with a fear so deep it might drown her. "Shaun. *Wake up.*"

Krieger snickered. The sorcerer spoke again.

Shaun's eyes finally focused on her. A cold smile crossed her lips. Sara took a step back.

Krieger was right. This was not Shaun. It was a cruel parody of everything Shaun had been to her, a puppet created to inflict pain and suffering.

Sara dropped her eyes from Shaun's, unable to look in them anymore and see a stranger staring back. The creature with Shaun's face took another step toward her. Sara took another step back. A feral need to run passed over her, but her knees struck the edge of the cot behind her, and she fell onto it.

Shaun's hands balled into fists.

Hot tears stung Sara's eyes and rolled down her face. They seemed to matter little to the creature in front of her. The creature's fists rose. Sara looked away, knowing what was about to come.

The Mordwellians had taken her father, her freedom, and now Shaun.

She was truly alone now.

ABOUT A.M. RYCROFT

A.M. Rycroft was born and raised in Pittsburgh, Pa.
She was accepted as a member of the Horror Writers
Association at the beginning of 2017 and won back to
back fantasy awards in the same year. She's also a die-hard
hockey and football fan.

Find out more about Rycroft and her worlds on her
website at www.writinginadarkroom.com or by following
her on Facebook (www.facebook.com/amrycroftwriter).

ACKNOWLEDGEMENTS

Many thanks to my beta readers and my editors for calling me on all my lazy and downright bad habits, for putting up with my numerous follow-up questions and requests for elaborations, and the last minute changes.

And my thanks to my spouse, who puts up with my weird hours, moods, and the creepy bits of flash fiction that pop into my head at the worst possible times. I'm honestly shocked you haven't run for the hills by now.

NOTES ABOUT
RIVEREND'S HISTORY

THE NINE YEARS WAR

The Tae Ahjin Empire once ruled over the lands around the Golden Peaks, just below the southern border of Cathell. Ten ruling houses shared equal responsibilities on the empire's council. But long-standing unrest between two houses—the House of Hahlerand and the House of Mackritae—brought civil war to the empire after the Hahlerand's ambassador was assassinated by a dark sorcerer in the Mackritae's service. Lines were drawn and the other eight houses chose sides and joined the conflict.

The Nine Years War ended when several of the houses grew weary of the bloodshed and split from the other sides in the conflict. The dissenting houses banded together to force the other houses into a peace accord that included dissolution of the empire.

All lands once held by the Tae Ahjin Empire were divided into ten separate kingdoms, one for each house. Ever after, the region became known as Decathea, or the Ten Kingdoms.

The House of Hahlerand chose lands on the eastern side of the Golden Peaks, at one end of the Kearning River, and called their kingdom Riverend. Unwilling to let their mortal enemies have full control of the Golden Peaks, the House of Mackritae took possession of the lands on the western side of the Golden Peaks and formed the kingdom of Mordwell.

The last thirty years have seen minor hostilities continue between the two kingdoms, despite the accord. Many a Riverend caravan has disappeared in the Golden Peaks' passes. Assassinations and child abductions committed against Riverend's ruling classes, via the dark magiks of Mordwell, forced the Hahlerands to declare a moratorium on magik in the kingdom, except for magik done as a healing art.

The ban persists to this day.

THE KNIGHTS SERVICE AND THE WATCHERS OF RIVEREND

The Knights Service is one of the most respected institutions in Riverend, responsible for creating not only the best fighters in the kingdom but the best strategic thinkers as well. The head of the service, the Knights Master, is the right hand of whomever rules the kingdom.

Application to the Knights Service is open to all citizens of good standing in Riverend, aged fourteen and older, regardless of birth or title. However, applicants must prove themselves through a series of physical and mental Trials. Only the top ten percent of applicants are approved by a board of three high-ranking knights who serve as the Trials' judges.

Once an applicant passes the Trials, they enter apprentice knight status. Apprenticeship lasts five years and consists of equal parts physical and academic training. Apprentice knights do not see combat on the battlefield until their fifth year.

After an uptick in assassination attempts and abductions by Mordwell, King Jaris increased the ranks of the King's Guard and expanded the responsibilities of select apprentice knights. Considered the most elite of the apprentice knights, Watchers are tasked with guarding family members of high-ranking officials and members of the Hahlerand family not in the immediate line of succession.

Apprentice knights can apply for admittance to the Watcher program as early as their second year. Acceptance is the highest honor an apprentice knight can achieve. Upon entry into the program, they must shadow an existing Watcher for a minimum of one year before being paired with a Ward of their own.

Watchers are expected to give their lives to protect their Ward, without question.

EXCERPT

CORRUPTION OF HONOR, PT. II

THE CROW
AND THE BUTTERFLY

THOMAS pulled her through the cobblestone streets, past broken storefronts and smoking remains. The acrid smoke drifting across the besieged city stung Shaun's nose and eyes. The gray woman who freed her from whatever dark spell she had been under followed them, seemingly unaffected by the scene.

Jak took the lead, running ahead of the group, sword in hand. He raised his free hand to his mouth and whistled, twice, in long bursts. A fallback signal. Other Riverend soldiers and knights broke off from the fighting and joined them as they fled through the city.

A dark figure suddenly burst out from behind a nearby building. It bowled over the soldiers at the front of the group and tackled Shaun. Another aimed for Thomas.

He shouted as he fell, "Biters!"

Shaun hit the ground with a sharp cry, pinned underneath the creature. It stared down at her with dead-white eyes and wheezed cold, fetid breath on her. A paralyzing sense that she had done this too many times before washed over her. Then the creature bit her shoulder, snapping her out of her daze.

The leather armor she wore kept the biter's teeth from penetrating her flesh, but the force of its gnawing made her cry out again. Cursing at the fiend, Shaun struggled against it as it dug its fingers into her arms. Even the rough fabric that covered part of them was no protection against the creature's icy touch.

Too weak to throw the biter off her, Shaun searched

for a weapon, but found none on her person or anywhere on the creature. It suddenly reared its head back and squealed in frustration. Then it opened its mouth wide and aimed for her unprotected face. A bolt of primal fear shot through her, followed by a hot wave that burned away the weakness in her limbs.

Without even thinking, her hand shot upward and slammed into the creature's jaw. The creature shook itself, spraying her with broken teeth and blood.

Before it could recover, Shaun punched it in the side of the head, knocking it off her. She pulled her knees to her chest, recoiled, and kicked the creature in its dead-pale face. It stumbled backward.

She got her feet under her again, rising from the hard cobblestone street. The fiend dove at her again, but she met it head on. Grabbing it by the throat, she forced it back while it snapped at her with the mess of bloody skin and bone that used to be its mouth.

Digging her boots in, Shaun rammed the creature back against the nearest building wall. The impact did not seem to faze it. It grabbed her bare wrists. She gritted her teeth against the creature's icy touch. The cold crawled up her arms and threatened to extinguish the fire inside her. The biter wheezed out something close to a laugh.

Growling, she fell back into a roll and pitched the creature over. It let go when it landed hard but jumped to its feet again unnaturally fast. She fell on it from behind, a step faster. Grabbing hold of its head, she twisted it as hard as she could. The creature's neck snapped with a satisfying crack. A grim smile crossed her face when the biter finally went limp.

The body fell from her grasp as the fire inside her suddenly blinked out without warning. Shaun stumbled backward, gasping, and fell to her knees. A cold sweat washed over her, leaving her shaking.

Thomas found her again and crouched next to her. His face was bruised and bloody from wounds he sustained while fighting the other creature. A sudden fear gripped her as a memory flashed through her mind, and she remembered what had happened to her on the road to Parna, after one of the creatures bit her leg.

She gasped out, "Did it bite you?"

He shook his head. "No. The others came to my aid before it could get its jaws on me." He nodded at the dead creature next to her. "How did you manage to do that on your own?"

Shaun also looked at it, slowly shaking her head. "I do not know."

Her eyes trailed down to herself, only then noticing the color of the leather armor covering her upper body and part of her upper arms. It was black, unlike anything Riverend soldiers wore. The shirt underneath was just as dark and the material was scratchier than a Riverend uniform shirt. Its sleeves ended just below her elbows, leaving her forearms and the black symbols tattooed on them exposed all the way down to her wrists.

She stared at the symbols. A memory of waking in a strange tent with those tattoos flashed through her mind. It felt more distant than the memory of being bitten by the creature in the woods, just after the fall of Riverend. But she remembered Sara was there when she woke.

When was that? *Where* was that?

Thomas laid a hand on her shoulder. "Shaun?"

She looked around, blinking, as she tried to make sense of the conflicting images in her head. "What's happening to me?"

***

Don't miss the exciting next installment, *The Crow and The Butterfly*, available wherever books are sold.

Made in the USA
Columbia, SC
10 August 2018